CATACOMB

J.F. PENN

This book is a work of fiction. The characters, incidents and dialogue are drawn from the author's imagination and are not to be construed as real. Any resemblance to actual events or persons, living or dead, is fictionalized or coincidental.

Catacomb
Copyright © J.F. Penn (2023). All rights reserved.

Paperback ISBN: 978-1-915425-34-8
Paperback Large Print ISBN: 978-1-915425-36-2
Ebook ISBN: 978-1-915425-33-1
Audiobook ISBN: 978-1-915425-35-5

The right of J.F. Penn to be identified as the author of this work has been asserted by the author in accordance with the Copyright, Designs and Patents Act,1988. All rights reserved. No part of this publication may be reproduced, stored in a retrieval system, or transmitted, in any form, or by any means, electronic, mechanical, photocopying, recording or otherwise, without the prior permission of the publishers.

This book is sold subject to the condition that it shall not, by way of trade or otherwise, be lent, resold, hired out, or otherwise circulated without the author's prior consent in any form of binding or cover other than that in which it is published and without a similar condition being imposed on the subsequent purchaser.

Requests to publish excerpts from this book, or media enquiries, should be sent to: joanna@JFPenn.com

Published by Curl Up Press

Cover and Interior Design: JD Smith
Composite images include some created by J.F. Penn with Midjourney

www.CurlUpPress.com

www.CurlUpPress.com

Till the monster stirred, that demon, that fiend

Grendel who haunted the moors, the wild

Marshes, and made his home in a hell.

Not hell but hell on earth.

—Beowulf

PROLOGUE

1,000 years ago

As the sun dipped below the horizon, it cast its final golden rays upon Castle Rock. The nascent settlement of Edinburgh stirred with a sense of foreboding as the shadows lengthened and bony fingers of darkness clawed at the walls of their humble homes. The chill of encroaching night swept through the village, a cloak of fear descending to silence any who might dare speak against the atrocity to come.

The dying light of day cast a sinister glow upon the gnarled and twisted trees that encircled the settlement, their skeletal branches swaying and groaning. A low, mournful wind wove its way through the ancient oaks, like the sorrowful cries of the damned.

A thick fog rose from the damp earth, slithering through the narrow lanes and curling around the huts of the settlement. It carried with it the acrid scent of decay, a pungent stench of rot and damp that seeped into the marrow of the villagers' bones.

As the hour of the ritual drew near, the villagers gathered together, seeking solace and strength in each other's company as, beneath them, an ancient force stirred.

Flora, a young mother, whispered a fervent prayer to the goddess as she cowered by her hearthside. Perhaps if she stayed inside, hidden, she would not have to witness what lay ahead. Her words were a plea for protection as the midnight hour approached, a time when the veil between the living and the dead was at its thinnest. Flora trembled as she clutched her baby girl, Ailsa, tight to her chest.

She had witnessed the price of defiance, the heavy burden that might threaten her precious child in years to come. To withhold an offering was to invite destruction upon their village, but she was terrified that her own blood might one day be demanded as payment.

As she rocked Ailsa, Flora reached out to touch the small clay pot that contained the ashes of her ancestors. They had done whatever they could to ensure the continuation of the village, and now Flora must do the same. She took a deep breath and walked outside to take her place amongst the gathering villagers.

The solemn drum beat began, the deep resonance marking the start of their annual abomination.

Ailsa, swaddled in a tattered woollen blanket, whimpered softly, sensing her mother's fear. Flora gently rocked the child, her eyes welling with tears as she stifled Ailsa's muffled cries so as not to draw attention.

A sliver of moonlight pierced the fog as the tribal elder led a procession through the narrow lane between the huts of the settlement. He was a hulking figure with a weathered face etched by time, like the rocky crags surrounding the village. Long, snow-white hair cascaded down his back, a stark contrast to the ritual cloak of tattered skins that hung heavily from his broad shoulders, used by generations of priests before him. He wore an obsidian talisman around his neck, the black stone seeming to draw the night inside it.

As the elder walked by, Flora looked up and met his piercing gaze. His eyes were the colour of storm clouds that held the weight of countless years of sacrifice and unspoken secrets. They seemed to bore into her soul, demanding unwavering loyalty and unspoken acquiescence to the ritual that was about to unfold. Flora looked away quickly, her heart pounding as she clutched Ailsa closer to her chest.

Behind the elder, two hooded priests walked at a deliberate, measured pace, carrying flaming torches held high. Their flickering light danced upon the damp earth, casting eerie, elongated shadows that seemed to twist and writhe like tortured souls.

Between the two torch-bearing priests, a slender young woman struggled to keep up with the sombre march. Her wrists were bound with coarse rope, the fibres rubbing her delicate skin to angry, red welts.

She stumbled on the uneven path, her bare feet bruised and bloodied by the jagged stones. With tear-streaked eyes, wide with terror, she desperately searched the faces of her kin for solace but found only downcast gazes and lips pressed tight with fear.

The young woman's once-lustrous auburn hair hung in matted, tangled strands, her once-vibrant green eyes now dull from the herbs she'd been given to ease the way ahead. Her ragged breaths were loud against the silence of the villagers, each gasp a second closer to her last.

As the priests passed by, the villagers joined the procession, walking behind with solemn steps in time with the drum.

They reached the outskirts of the settlement, where the oppressive darkness of night seemed to coalesce and gather, hungry and expectant. The ground beneath their feet grew rougher, slick with moisture from the ever-present fog that clung to the earth like a spectral shroud. The air grew colder, heavy with the dank scent of decay and the metallic tang of blood that saturated the soil upon which they trod.

At the outer boundary of the village, a jagged, imposing

rock loomed from the earth, its gnarled surface covered with layers of moss and lichen, marking the entrance to a dark and foreboding cave. The wind howled a mournful dirge as it swept past the entrance, carrying with it the whispers of restless souls who haunted this unholy place.

In the flickering torchlight, the elder raised his arms, his tattered cloak billowing around him like the wings of a malevolent bird. He chanted ancient words passed down through generations, a sombre incantation in a language long forgotten by all but the most devout practitioners of their dark rites.

The villagers, compelled by fear and tradition, hesitantly joined in. Their voices wove together to form a mournful chorus that echoed across the darkened landscape.

As the chanting reached a crescendo, the elder led the young woman to the jagged rock and secured her to its cold, unforgiving surface.

Her cries of desperation echoed within the cave entrance as the skies above swirled with menacing clouds. The air grew thick and a roll of thunder boomed out from the approaching storm. The wind howled like a beast in torment, its voice carrying the echoes of a thousand anguished cries, heralding the approach of the ancient creature.

From the depths of the earth, the Grendsluagh emerged.

It was a monstrous abomination born of darkness and chaos. Its vast form was a grotesque fusion of man and demon, an unholy testament to its malevolent power. The creature's skin was the colour of a tar pit, slick and oozing with a foul ichor that glistened in the flickering torchlight. Towering above the trembling villagers, its hulking body was a twisted mass of sinew and muscle, contorted limbs ending in jagged, razor-sharp talons that gouged the earth.

Its misshapen head bore a twisted mockery of what once might have been a human face, its features warped and elongated into a snarling mask of rage and hunger.

The Grendsluagh's eyes were soulless, twin orbs of black that seemed to drain what was left of the light. Its mouth, a gaping maw filled with rows of jagged, yellowed teeth, dripped with an acrid saliva that hissed and sizzled as it met the dirt beneath.

As it loomed over the sacrifice, it gave a guttural growl, a sound torn from the bowels of the earth.

The elder and priests increased the tempo of their fervent chanting, beseeching the creature to accept the offering and spare the village from its wrath.

The Grendsluagh turned away from the lone sacrifice.

It looked at the gathered villagers and took a step toward them with malevolent intent. Flora gasped, holding Ailsa more tightly against her chest, as she tried to stop herself from fleeing. To attract attention now — from the creature or the elder — might only serve to seal their fate in blood.

The elder spoke ancient words of power as he lifted the obsidian talisman high.

The Grendsluagh reeled back with a growl, snarling with rage — but it turned away from the villagers.

It reached for the terrified young woman and ripped her from the rock with its massive, clawed hands. The Grendsluagh's grip closed around her with a sickening crunch, the force of its grasp shredding the rope that bound her to the rock like mere thread.

As it dragged her struggling and writhing form into the cave, the Grendsluagh's grotesque silhouette was briefly illuminated by the torchlight, casting monstrous shadows that merged with the darkness beyond.

The villagers averted their eyes. They could not bear witness to the horror that unfolded before them as the night was pierced by the young woman's final, anguished scream.

Once the echo of her cries had faded into darkness, the villagers returned to their homes, the weight of the ritual heavy upon their hearts. Tonight they would grieve the dead, but tomorrow they would feast to celebrate the living.

As Flora tucked Ailsa into her nest of blankets, she kissed the tiny girl's forehead and sent up a prayer of gratitude to the goddess.

In the coming months, the fields would deliver a bountiful harvest and their animals would remain healthy and multiply. The young mothers would deliver without fear of death in childbirth, and the settlement would grow richer and more prosperous.

At least for another year.

CHAPTER 1

The Edinburgh theatre was a relic of an age gone by, its Victorian grandeur now faded, but still retaining an ethereal charm. The stage was a world in itself where stories came to life, where characters breathed and words written centuries ago still inspired the enraptured audience.

Walker Kane stood at the back, a solitary figure in the dimmed auditorium, his gaze riveted on the stage as he watched his daughter perform. The audience knew her as the compassionate, sheltered Miranda, daughter of the banished Prospero in Shakespeare's *The Tempest*, but to him, she would always be his little girl, Emily.

At first glance, Walker appeared nondescript, just another man in the crowd. He wore a pair of well-worn jeans that hugged his lean frame, paired with a black leather jacket that bore the battered marks of time. His dark hair was cropped short with specks of white at his temples, and day-old stubble framed his angular jaw.

But his eyes were those of a man who had seen too much. They were an intense steel grey, with a flash of danger, a silent warning, lingering in their depths.

His hands, large and capable, bore the imprints of his past. Scars crisscrossed his rough skin, a map of every rescue mission, each dangerous extraction, and every life he had pulled from the jaws of death. Down the side of his neck, barely visible above the collar of his jacket, was the puckered trail of a burn. An ugly reminder of a near-death experience, a mission that had gone terribly wrong, trapping him underground in a burning tomb. The scar wound its path down his body, hidden under layers of clothing but always present in its reminder of a past he wished he could forget.

As Emily performed her lines with grace, Walker remembered when she used to prance around their old living room, a makeshift stage for her childhood antics and a precursor to the acting career she now pursued.

"O, brave new world, that has such people in it!"

Emily's speech as Miranda resonated with emotion, carrying a pitch-perfect blend of hope and innocence. Walker heard in it an echo of the girl she once was, and the woman she was fast becoming. He stifled a sigh. How many years had he missed that he could never get back?

His military service had been a tempest of its own, a maelstrom of violence and despair that he'd refused to let touch his daughter. And yet, standing in the shadows of the theatre, he wondered if his absence had inadvertently summoned its own kind of storm in her life.

As the last act of *The Tempest* came to a close, the curtain fell on the final scene and the theatre erupted into applause. Walker joined in, clapping until his palms stung.

The curtain came back up, and the actors walked on stage for a bow.

Emily stood hand in hand with the young actor who'd played Ferdinand, the chemistry between them undeniable. As she glanced up at him with mischief in her eyes, Walker wondered what else he didn't know about his daughter's life.

The final curtain came down, and the theatre began to empty. The worn-out velvet seats creaked as people rose. The cacophony of chatter filled the air; the heavy scent of perfume mingled with the musty smell of the old theatre.

Walker made his way outside and around the back of the theatre to the stage door.

It was a balmy night and the excitement of the festival that captivated the city every summer was in full swing. A small crowd of family, friends, and well-wishers eagerly awaited the actors. They chattered and laughed together, some swigging from bottles of prosecco or craft beer as preparations began for the night of celebration ahead.

Amongst the crowd, a familiar face stood out.

Maggie, Walker's ex-wife, with Bill, her husband of more than a decade. Their arms were casually draped around each other in a familiar embrace. They seemed happy, content in a way that Walker could only remember as a faint glimmer from the past he had run from.

Time had etched its presence on Maggie's face, softening the sharp angles of her youth to a mature beauty. But Walker could still see the vibrant woman he had fallen in love with so long ago, and the echoes of her in Emily now.

Maggie's gaze was focused on the stage door as she chatted with Bill, his quiet words eliciting a laugh that rang out in the evening air. She used to laugh like that with him years ago, but Walker had left to protect both her and Emily — at least that's what he told himself back then.

Over the years, Maggie had sent him pictures of Emily, and Walker was grateful for her attempt to keep the dying embers of their connection alive. He had been a ghost, lingering on the outskirts of their lives, too tangled in the adrenalin of constant missions to realise what he was losing as the days ticked past.

A part of him ached at the sight of Maggie's happiness, a sharp reminder of what he'd given up. But the better part of him was glad to see her smile, glad that she had found someone who could be there for her and Emily. Walker couldn't make up for the past, but perhaps he could now build on the embers of what he'd burned down.

The stage door creaked open, revealing a group of actors basking in the afterglow of their successful performance. Emily stood among them, her fingers interlaced with those of the young man from the stage, their shared triumph evident in their beaming smiles.

A burst of applause erupted from the crowd as the actors walked out to join the well-wishers. Emily and her boyfriend walked straight to her mother.

Maggie enveloped Emily in a warm hug. "Congratulations, Petal! You were fantastic — and you too, Tom." Maggie put a hand out to touch the young man's arm. "I hope you can have a wonderful evening celebrating together."

Walker's heart beat faster as he heard Maggie say Emily's nickname. They had started calling her that when she had eaten May cherry blossom petals as a baby, her chubby fingers stroking the soft pink as she chuckled with happiness.

He reached into his pocket, his fingers brushing against the small jewellery box nestled within.

It contained a locket, a delicate piece he had chosen carefully for Emily's eighteenth birthday and engraved for her. But was it appropriate? Would she even be happy to see him here?

Walker had often faced uncertainty in his line of duty, but this was different. This was personal, a battle with his own fear and insecurity. He was trained to face enemies and overcome obstacles, but now he was as vulnerable as a ship caught in a tempest, unable to find a way ahead.

He clutched the jewellery box a little tighter, the sharp edges pressing against his palm. He couldn't leave without seeing Emily. He had to step back into her world, regardless of the outcome.

With a final, steadying breath, Walker stepped out of the shadows and made his way toward the family group, his stride purposeful.

Maggie saw him first.

Her eyes widened in surprise, then confusion and concern. "Walker? I… didn't know you were coming."

Emily turned, and a shadow of uncertainty flickered across her features. "Dad?" The word was a hesitant question, a cautious hope.

Then, as if the clouds had parted to reveal the sun, her expression transformed. The uncertainty dissolved, replaced by a radiant happiness that took Walker's breath away.

"Dad!" Emily said once more, the single word carrying so much weight.

The world seemed to pause in that moment, the noise and the crowd fading away. All Walker could see was Emily, her face illuminated with a joy that was directed solely at him. It was a moment Walker wished he could capture, a snapshot of happiness that was as fragile as it was beautiful.

Emily took two steps toward him and then she was in his arms, hugging him as he pulled her close and kissed her hair.

Walker nodded his thanks to Maggie and Bill over her shoulder as they stood back to allow some privacy for the reunion.

"You were a wonderful Miranda," Walker said as they pulled apart. "I loved the play."

Emily blushed a little and then turned to introduce the young actor at her side. "Dad, this is Tom. Tom, this is my dad, Walker."

Tom extended a hand, and they shook with a firm grip.

"Emily told me you're in the military."

Walker nodded. "Yes, search and rescue. Well, I was. I'm… taking a break right now."

The words triggered a sudden onslaught of memory.

The darkness of an ancient tomb, the air thick with dust. Ominous rumbling, then a lethal rain of rock and earth as the walls caved in. Echoes of terrified screams. Cries abruptly silenced as his team was lost, their blood draining into the desert like so many before them, an offering to ancient gods that still demanded sacrifice.

Walker blinked, forcefully pulling himself out of the memory, back into the moment.

Desperate to shift the sombre mood, he reached into his pocket and pulled out the jewellery box, offering it to Emily. "Happy birthday, I know it's a few days late…"

Emily waved his apology away and took the box. "Thank you. It's good of you to come."

She opened the box. Nestled within the velvet lining was a gold locket in the shape of an intricate Celtic knot, a looped pattern that symbolised the eternity of life — and love.

"It's beautiful." Emily lifted the locket from the box, the delicate chain dangling from her fingers as she read the inscription on the back. *For Emily — Love, Dad.*

"Thanks so much, Dad. It's beautiful, but I won't wear it right now." She gestured to her skinny jeans and silver sequined top. "It doesn't really go with my outfit. But I love it, really. We're going to burlesque at the Spiegeltent tonight, but maybe we can catch up tomorrow or something?"

"Of course. I've put my new number on a card in the jewellery box. Call me when you're up tomorrow, and we'll have coffee or something. Have a great night."

Emily smiled, and Walker's heart lifted at the warmth in her eyes. Perhaps it really could be possible to rebuild their relationship.

Emily walked over to her mother and planted a warm kiss on Maggie's cheek before stepping back. With a final wave, she and Tom walked away, their arms around each other.

They were a picture of carefree young love, but as they moved further from the theatre's halo of light, it seemed to Walker that they were swallowed by encroaching shadow.

CHAPTER 2

As the noise of the festival rang out over Edinburgh, Laurel March approached the university.

Its ancient stones loomed in silhouette against the star-dappled sky, its structure imbued with centuries of knowledge, a testament to the city's storied past. But it held secrets too, and Laurel was determined to find them.

Curiosity had always driven her to take risks. Her father had once said there was never a loop she didn't want to close. But what was life, if not an adventure into knowledge? Sometimes, it was worth taking a risk to find the truth, and so, here she was, creeping around at night, chasing a whisper of a possibility of a fragment of a rumour.

Laurel picked her way carefully across the cobblestone courtyard and slipped through a back entrance of the university.

The air was heavy with the musty scent of books and aged wood as the labyrinth of knowledge stretched out into the shadows before her. Moonlight filtering through the tall, Gothic windows bathed the room in a spectral glow, which lent an eerie atmosphere to her forbidden exploration.

But that was probably because she had been reading way too much Lovecraft recently.

Laurel worked here in the daytime as one of the many

librarians, but the university library was a different place by night. The grand arches and high ceilings, so familiar and inviting during the day, now loomed above her and stretched into a darkness filled with shifting shadows.

She tried to walk silently, but her footsteps still echoed softly in the cavernous space. In her usual black clothes and carrying only a small backpack, Laurel blended with the shadows of the library, but as she crossed a moonbeam, the faint illumination caught her flame-red curls, tied back with a ribbon as dark as midnight.

A multitude of tattoos adorned her skin. They started at her wrists, coiling like serpents up her toned arms, each symbol a story etched in ink.

On her left forearm, a vivid depiction of the Celtic Tree of Life, its roots intertwined, symbolising the interconnectedness of all life. The owl of the Greek goddess Athena, a symbol of wisdom, nestled in its branches. On her right arm, a stylised representation of the Hindu goddess Kali, dancing with her cycle of time and destruction.

Each image was a testament to Laurel's love for myth and legend and her hunger for knowledge. The desire to always know more. This drive had led to her career as a librarian, most recently here at the university. Her position gave her access to much that fed her curiosity, but sometimes, she had to bend the rules a little to discover what lay behind the official version of the truth.

As she walked past the towering stacks of books, her fingers brushed lightly against the dusty spines. The faint scent of aged parchment and ink, the perfume of centuries of accumulated wisdom, filled her senses. Laurel was at home here, and libraries had always been her sanctuary.

The books were a fortress against the outside world, and every one she read became a brick in the wall that shielded her from the slings and arrows of modern life. Which, to be honest, she would rather avoid, despite the fact her mother was always dropping hints about wanting grandchildren.

Laurel loved to follow breadcrumbs of knowledge to new discoveries. Last week, she had assisted an architectural student in digging out some old plans of the university from the archives.

She couldn't help but pore over them herself once he had finished for the day. Cartography was one of her many passions, and she had traced the lines of the library with care as she considered how much history lay beneath the place she worked every day.

But she had found something curious on one old map that had been left off modern plans of the university.

A hidden room.

And tonight, she was determined to find it.

Laurel reached the back of the library and pulled out her phone to examine the photos of the old map. The entrance had to be around here somewhere.

Putting her phone away and pulling out a small torch, she searched the area, examining the stacks for hidden levers or moveable shelves. She was meticulous and patient, having been raised on a steady diet of mystery novels and detective films that made her certain she'd find an entrance somewhere.

If there was a hidden room, there was a hidden door.

Finally, she spotted a bookshelf that, unlike the others nearby, stood a little distance from the stone wall. The shelves were heavy with volumes on the history of tax legislation, but behind them she spotted wood rather than stone. Laurel smiled in triumph as she slipped into the alcove behind the shelf and tried the old oak door.

It was locked.

She felt around the frame looking for a key as she examined the door. It didn't look like anything special and it would be just her luck if it was a maintenance closet, but something told her it was more than that.

She walked out of the alcove and returned to the stack of

tax legislation. If this had been her secret door, she would keep a key somewhere close, somewhere no one would look.

Laurel pulled over a ladder from one of the other stacks and climbed a few steps so she could read the higher levels.

She squinted at the tiny writing as she scanned the thick spines, then noticed one book that was less dusty than the others. One that looked as if it had been opened recently.

The Malt Tax Act of 1725.

Laurel frowned. Surely that would not warrant such regular reading.

She reached up and pulled it down, opening the thick volume to find a hollowed-out chamber within its pages.

And a set of two keys.

They were modern, as if they could belong to a janitor's cupboard, but now, Laurel was sure it was nothing of the sort.

She walked back around to the door, unlocked it, and pushed it open.

Laurel couldn't help a smile of triumph at her discovery as she continued inside.

It looked like it had once been an intimate chapel. It had a vaulted ceiling, and pillars flanked a stone altar at one end. But this was a chapel dedicated to no god Laurel recognised.

The walls were adorned with murals of the history of Edinburgh, but beside the stone and brick buildings were otherworldly creatures — beings of myth and nightmare. The artistry was hauntingly beautiful, even as the grotesque forms seemed to writhe and flicker in her torchlight. The cityscape was almost lifelike, each brick and cobblestone meticulously crafted, but this city existed in a monstrous alternate history. What was this place?

Laurel moved deeper into the room.

The weak light of her torch illuminated gold-embossed spines of books in one niche, their unusual titles a tantalising promise of hidden secrets. The scent of ancient vellum and parchment pervaded the air, alongside the unmistakable smell of centuries-old ink.

There was a large table in the centre of the room, an ornately carved piece of mahogany with a dark patina. An oversized volume bound in worn, almost black leather lay on the top with a title in gold leaf: *Codex of the Cabal and the Monstrous Accord.*

A title so curious that Laurel couldn't resist.

She opened the book.

The yellowing pages were filled with elegant calligraphy recording a list of years alongside names of Edinburgh's most powerful and affluent citizens going back centuries. There were other names listed too, although sometimes only the words female or male. The edges and corners of each page were illustrated with strange carnivorous plants with razor-sharp thorns and the face of a monster drawn over and over again from different angles, all portraying a nightmare come to life.

Laurel turned to the end of the inscribed pages.

The name at the end of the list with the current date was the chancellor of the university, Dr Darcel Knox. Technically, her boss. Or at least her boss's boss.

Laurel frowned as she regarded the book. Who else was part of this 'Cabal' and what was their 'monstrous accord'? Was this some glorified old boys' club, or was it something far more sinister?

The sudden creak of a door shattered the silence of the library.

Laurel's heart lurched in her chest. She froze, straining to listen as a low murmur of deep voices drifted in from the shadowed corridors beyond.

The voices were drawing closer, resonating baritone notes punctuated by the rhythmic cadence of footfalls on wood, the sound amplified by the high-vaulted ceiling.

They were coming this way.

CHAPTER 3

Panic surged through Laurel. Her breath hitched in her throat as she hurried back to the door and quietly eased it shut to at least partially disguise her entry.

She scanned the room for a hiding place.

There was a nook in one corner, obscured by heavy velvet curtains, their deep burgundy hue almost black in the dim light.

She hurried over and slipped behind the drapes, pressing her body against the cold, damp wall as she tried to calm her breathing. The fabric was thick and heavy against her skin, the musty smell of age and dust filling her nostrils. She prayed she wouldn't sneeze.

The door opened.

Laurel hardly dared breathe as two sets of footsteps entered the room.

"I'm sure I locked the door yesterday, but then I'm sure I had my speech notes with me, too." A huff of impatience. "Age brings its many challenges."

The voice was unmistakably familiar. The chancellor, Dr Darcel Knox.

His inflection was as crisp as dry parchment, and his tone carried an undercurrent of authority that could command a room, as he regularly did for his many speeches.

His walrus moustache was a source of amusement for the younger members of his staff, but they would never dare mock him in public.

"Ah, here they are. And presumably the other key is on my desk, where I thought my notes were."

The footsteps came closer to her hiding place.

Laurel froze, her breathing light and shallow.

A rustle of papers.

The footsteps moved away again before the chancellor spoke once more. "The sacrifice must be tonight, Hamish. Any longer and we risk losing everything."

The second man — Hamish — had a rough voice, like the grinding of gravel. "Shall I get the usual team to pick up someone from the dregs of the festival?"

"I actually have someone in mind. My son's latest girl. Pretty enough, but not suitable for our lineage. Comes from a common family, a broken home, and she's encouraging Tom to… *act*."

The disdain was evident in the chancellor's tone.

Hamish gave a low chuckle. "Won't he object to her as your choice?"

Their footsteps moved back toward the door.

"Tom will do as I say and he'll find another girl, a better girl, soon enough. Take her quickly, though. The sacrifice must be done before the dawn breaks."

"Of course. I'll meet you in the Chamber of Offering at three a.m."

The two men left the room, closing the door behind them and locking it before walking away. Their footsteps gradually faded into silence.

Laurel let out a shaky breath and waited until she was sure they were gone before she emerged from behind the curtain.

She turned on her torch again and rushed over to the door, checking she could still get out. The key turned in the lock and she was free — she should just leave the library, pretend she was never there, forget this unholy chapel.

But the chancellor's words — and the young woman's fate — echoed in her mind.

Laurel turned back to examine a mural on the walls. One haunting depiction now took on a new significance.

A tribe of people stood before a hulking beast, its form swirling and shifting, as if formed from the darkness itself. A lone woman knelt before the creature, her limbs bound with rope, her features frozen in terror as it reached for her with taloned claws.

Under the mural, a single word: Grendsluagh.

It must be the name for the creature, and it brought to Laurel's mind Grendel, the mythical monster of the Beowulf legend, combined with the *sluagh*, restless spirits of the Celtic dead.

The style of the painting resembled ecclesiastical artwork. The creature took the place of a deity, the worshippers and sacrifice reminiscent of religious congregation and ritual. But it was a perversion of faith, an ancient blood sacrifice that — judging by the words of the chancellor — continued into the present day.

How could this be possible in modern Edinburgh?

The room seemed to close in around Laurel as her weak torchlight cast long, grotesque shadows that danced and writhed on the stone walls, bringing the creature to a semblance of life.

She shook her head to clear the vision. She had to learn more.

Laurel walked over to the stone altar. An ancient wooden chest sat on top, adorned with the intricate carvings of a Celtic triskelion symbol, three curling arms etched into the wood. They seemed to writhe and twist under her gaze; the lines ebbed and flowed like the tide. Intertwined with each arm were monstrous faces, their expressions twisted into perpetual snarls.

She reached out and opened the chest.

Inside, nestled on a bed of faded crimson velvet, lay a small book. Next to it, a long slim piece of black rock with a hole in one end, as if designed to be worn. Its darkness was so absolute it seemed to swallow the light, giving the stone an otherworldly aura.

Laurel picked it up.

Its weight was surprising, heavier than a rock its size had any right to be. She turned it over in her hands, feeling its smooth surface. It looked like obsidian, volcanic glass formed from rapidly cooling lava. But why was it here, and what significance did it hold?

She put it down and examined the book.

It was small, fitting snugly within her palm as she picked it up. The cover was rough against her fingertips, the texture reminiscent of antique leather. She swallowed hard, pushing aside the nauseating thought that it could be human skin.

As Laurel carefully opened it, the faint scent of mould and decay wafted up from its brittle pages. It was yellowed with age and filled with hand-drawn sketches and cryptic writing by a long-dead hand. A labyrinthine catacomb sprawled across several pages, its intricate design twisting and turning back upon itself as it wound down into the earth below the city.

Sketches of creatures, each more horrifying than the last, were entwined within the catacomb's design. Skittering mutants with too many eyes, humanoid figures with elongated arms, and writhing masses of bony spiders with cadaverous limbs.

Laurel traced the path leading down to the heart of the catacomb, its network of tunnels and chambers carved down into the ancient volcano on which Edinburgh stood. It had last erupted over 350 million years ago, and its power was thought to lie dormant. But could there be another ecosystem down there, evolving within the caves away from the city?

The path was a descent into the unknown, a journey to the monster in its depths. A journey that a young woman would face tonight — unless Laurel could stop the sacrifice.

The thought crossed her mind, and she immediately dismissed it. How could she possibly hope to stand against a clandestine Cabal that held such power, a society that had clearly orchestrated these monstrous rituals for centuries?

But she couldn't tear her gaze from the mural of the sacrifice and a lump formed in her throat at the chancellor's scornful words, his casual dismissal of a life he deemed unworthy.

A spark of determination flickered within her.

Although Laurel might not be able to bring down the Cabal entirely, she could at least warn the young woman they were targeting.

But she had to hurry.

She took some pictures of the room and the mural on her phone, then stuffed the book and the obsidian object into her pack as evidence against the Cabal.

She cast a final glance at the monstrous depiction of the Grendsluagh and shook her head. "You will not have your sacrifice tonight."

Laurel hurried out of the hidden room, locked the door, and put the key back in the tax book, before heading back out into the city.

If the chancellor's son, Tom, was an actor, he would likely be performing at one of the festival events. Tonight, the city was alive with celebration and festivities; the streets were filled with students and townsfolk alike, their attention diverted. It would be all too easy to make a young woman disappear amid the chaos.

Shaking off her apprehension, Laurel set off, jogging toward the heart of the festivities. She had to find Tom and this girl in time.

CHAPTER 4

The Spiegeltent's atmosphere buzzed with excitement as Emily and Tom stepped inside, their hands entwined.

Spotlights cast a kaleidoscope of light over the gathered crowd. The air was thick with the scent of spilled wine and a heady mix of perfume and the musky undertone of passion. It was a world of seductive decadence, where shadows and secrets danced together.

Onstage, a burlesque performer moved with hypnotic grace, her tight costume rippling like midnight clouds come to life as she undulated to the heavy bass of the music. Her features were highlighted with stark, dramatic makeup, her eyes smouldering with alluring intensity as she wove a spell over the mesmerised crowd.

As they pushed toward the stage, Emily tried to lose herself in the performance, but her thoughts kept drifting back to the unexpected encounter with her father.

She touched the jewellery box in her pocket as she considered the years he had missed. She didn't know him at all — and for many years, she hadn't even wanted to know him — but perhaps this was a new start.

Tom sensed her distraction and leaned in close, his warm breath tickling her ear as he whispered, "Are you okay, Em?"

She looked up, the concern in his gaze momentarily pulling her back to the present.

"Yeah, I'm fine. Just thinking about my dad, that's all."

Tom ran his hand gently down her back, his thumb tracing circles on her skin. "You can see him tomorrow. Let's you and me have fun tonight." The suggestion in his voice made Emily shiver in anticipation.

She pushed aside all thoughts of her father and allowed herself to be swept up in the vibrant, sensual world of the Spiegeltent, the music and movement offering a temporary escape from memories of the past.

The burlesque dancer on stage held the gaze of the audience with an unflinching intensity, her eyes dark and knowing, as if she could see into the souls of those who watched. Her movements were a potent mix of fluid grace and raw power, her body undulating to the frenzied cheers of the crowd and the music, each twist and turn a breathtaking display of control and abandon.

Emily found herself drawn to the dancer, admiring the woman's fierce confidence and her ability to hold the audience's attention. Emily was trying to channel that same power in her acting career, and there was so much to learn.

The dancer executed her final, dramatic flourish, and the crowd erupted into applause. The spotlight dimmed, and the music segued into a new beat, leaving the audience breathless and wanting more.

Tom's phone buzzed in his pocket.

He pulled it out and, as he looked at it, a shadow crossed his face. "It's my dad. I need to get this. I'll just go outside to speak to him. I'll bring you a drink on the way back. I won't be long."

He bent to kiss her cheek and then slipped into the crowd.

As Emily watched the next act, she considered what

Tom's father might want. The Knoxes were an old and affluent family. They lived in one of Edinburgh's grandest old houses, nestled in a wealthy neighbourhood where prestige was everything. His father was the chancellor of the university, but the man's influence seemed to reach much further, casting a long shadow over the city and beyond.

Tom had followed a passion for acting, a career that his father vehemently disapproved of. To the elder man, acting was a frivolous pursuit, a deviation from the distinguished legacy he had built and expected his son to uphold. He wanted Tom in academia, or at least law or banking, a career suitable for the family name.

Emily had only once been to the Knox house, a labyrinthine mansion that bristled with an air of restrained opulence. The walls whispered secrets, and the cold, unyielding gaze of ancestral portraits seemed to follow her every move.

When they had entered that night, a little drunk from a college event, Tom's father stood on the grand marble staircase above them, gazing down with unsettling intensity, his unspoken judgment covering her like an icy shroud.

After a minute, he turned without saying a word and walked away into shadow.

Emily had stayed that one night, but since then, Tom had come to her student room in shared accommodation. It wasn't much, but at least they had the freedom to do as they pleased.

As much as Tom denied his father's influence on his choices, Emily couldn't help but feel a twinge of unease, a nagging doubt that nestled in the back of her mind. Did Tom share his father's views, even if only in some small, hidden part of himself? After all, he was an actor with a raw talent. Like a chameleon, he could play the lover and the villain with equal passion, a transition she had seen him embody on stage.

If Emily was honest, she had glimpsed a darker side to

him. Sometimes in the midst of passion, he gripped her neck too tight as he pushed inside, her breathless gasps driving him into a frenzy. But then he kissed her and held her close and said all the right words. Perhaps his edge of danger was part of the attraction, and she certainly craved his touch tonight.

A few minutes later, Tom pushed his way through the crowd, his expression stormy, an open bottle of beer in each hand.

He gave one to Emily and clinked his drink against hers before taking several gulps. He turned to watch the dancers, a shadow in his gaze.

Emily was used to his darker moods after he spoke with his father, but Tom usually snapped out of it soon enough. She took a long pull of her own beer and then another.

They finished the drinks quickly and danced together, undulating with the music, fuelled by the energy of the crowd. Tom's hands weaved a trail of fire across her skin.

The music grew louder; the bass reverberated through Emily's body, her heart pumping with its rhythm. The colours in the Spiegeltent grew more intense, their hues deepening and pulsating in time with the music.

Emily felt the world around her start to spin. She wasn't much of a drinker, but it was only one beer. This sensation felt different, somehow.

As her vision narrowed, the crowd blurred and shifted, their faces and forms morphing into something more akin to creatures than human beings. Twisted shapes of sinister, otherworldly beings lurked at the periphery of her vision, emerging from the walls of the Spiegeltent, their outlines wavering and indistinct, as if they were both there and not there at the same time.

Panic clawed at Emily's chest, her heartbeat pounding in her ears as she tried to make sense of the surreal world that had engulfed her.

She reached out for Tom, her fingers trembling as they sought his steady presence.

As her hand closed around his, she looked up into his dark eyes, searching for reassurance in the midst of the swirling chaos.

She tried to speak, but her lips were numb, her throat tightening.

Tom leaned in close, his voice barely audible above the din of the music. "I'm so sorry, Em, but my father…" His voice trailed off, but in his gaze was a mix of regret and dark promise. "Just relax now. Let's go outside."

Emily felt heavy, weighed down as if her limbs were out of her control, as Tom forced her through the crowd toward the exit.

CHAPTER 5

Laurel hurried through the Princes Street Gardens toward the Spiegeltent. The sound of raucous laughter, clinking glasses, and the throb of bass-heavy music spilled out from the venue, mingling with the chatter of the crowd that ebbed and flowed around it.

Normally, she would have enjoyed the revelry and debauched atmosphere, the blend of bohemian and burlesque. But tonight, Laurel had only one goal.

She had used social media to track pictures of Tom and his girlfriend, Emily, through other members of *The Tempest* production. The most recent images were taken only twenty minutes earlier at the Spiegeltent, and Laurel could only hope the couple were still there.

The venue was a vortex of wanton chaos; the scent of sweat and booze and an underlying metallic tang of excitement swirled around her as she entered. Indigo and crimson lights spun over the crowd as it surged with the barely restrained energy of misrule.

But Laurel barely registered the surrounding spectacle. She scanned the crowd. The sea of faces was a blur of colour and movement, with surreal snapshots of celebration as the lights strobed each moment into a memory.

She fought her way through the mass of people and climbed a pillar at one side to get a better view.

There they were.

On the far side of the tent, in the midst of the undulating crowd, Tom was leading Emily toward the exit. His arm was tight around her waist as she sagged against him. Intoxicated, perhaps, but certainly unaware of her fate.

"Emily!" Laurel shouted — but her voice was lost in the din of the music.

She jumped off the pillar and elbowed her way across the tent and through the tumultuous crowd.

She had to reach them in time.

* * *

As Tom guided her outside the Spiegeltent, Emily fought against the heaviness in her limbs.

Her instinct screamed at her to break free, but Tom's grip around her waist was like a vice. She had revelled in his strength when he lifted her in his arms as a lover, but now his iron embrace terrified her.

He forced her away from the Spiegeltent, toward a shadowed copse of trees with a road beyond. Edinburgh Castle loomed above them like a dark omen, its ancient stones silhouetted against the night sky as storm clouds gathered in the distance.

With each step, Emily's desperation grew, her heart pounding like a drumbeat in her chest.

She thought of her father, his promise to meet her tomorrow. If only he were here right now. Tom would not dare touch her if Walker were by her side. Her father was military, his abilities in combat and search and rescue far more developed than his relationship skills. Whatever his past failures as a father, he would know what to do.

Forcing herself to concentrate and break through the haze of whatever drugs Tom had dosed her with, she inched her hand to her pocket.

She reached for the small jewellery box.

As her fingers closed around it, she stumbled a little to hide her movement, pulling it from her pocket and letting it fall to the ground. Emily sent up a silent prayer to a god she didn't believe in. *Please let him find it.*

Tom urged Emily on, and as they reached the road, a black van appeared from the street opposite. Its engine idled as the side door slid open.

The interior was shrouded in darkness, a gaping void that swallowed all light and hope. Tom's grip tightened on Emily's waist as he forced her inside.

She fell to the cold metal floor, breath ragged, heart pounding, vaguely aware of two other men within the van.

As the prick of a needle pierced her neck and she sank into blackness, Emily's last thought was of her father. *Find me, Dad. Please.*

* * *

Laurel raced out of the dizzying clamour of the Spiegeltent, but it had taken too long to get through so many revellers. As she scanned the dimly lit park for any sign of Tom and Emily, they were nowhere to be seen.

A group of students stood smoking and drinking from cans of craft beer.

Laurel called over, "Did you see a couple just leave here?"

Most of them replied with slurred words and vague gestures, but one pointed into a copse of trees. "Maybe that way?"

It was all she had to go on. Laurel sprinted away and raced through the trees.

As she emerged on the other side, she saw a black van on the road ahead. Tom, his face illuminated by a streetlight, pushed Emily inside.

"Stop!" Laurel shouted, but Tom climbed in. The door slammed shut, and the van drove away.

She was too late.

She pulled out her phone, snapping pictures as the van picked up speed, but it was too far and the licence plate was illegible.

Laurel stood by the road, her mind whirling.

She could go to the police. She had the book and pictures from the secret chapel — but no, the chancellor's influence was far-reaching. They would likely just brush her off as a paranoid librarian, high on myth and festival excess. She could already imagine the skeptical looks, the dismissive nods.

Any investigation would be too slow to save Emily.

But it was her only option. She couldn't go into the catacomb alone and she had to do something.

As Laurel turned to walk back through the park toward the nearest police station, she noticed a small object in the grass.

A jewellery box.

She picked it up and opened it.

Nestled within was a golden locket, the delicate chain glinting under the light from the streetlamp. Engraved on its surface were the words *For Emily — Love, Dad.*

Emily must have dropped it as she fought to get away.

Tucked under the locket was a card with a phone number.

Laurel pulled out her phone and hoped like hell that this man would take her seriously.

CHAPTER 6

THE DISTANT HUM OF the Edinburgh Festival punctuated the warm night air, a testament to the city's vibrant life above ground. But Maxine Mbaye understood that the shadows of the subterranean world provided far more freedom to roam.

She hoisted herself out of the access hole, her muscles straining as she quickly thrust the heavy metal cover back into place.

Her slim, wiry frame, honed from years of urban exploration, was streaked with grime and dust. She hoisted a worn backpack over her shoulder as she hurried across the cobblestones of a quiet street into an ancient churchyard, its tombstones standing sentinel in the moonlit summer night.

Max looked around, making sure that no one had seen her. Satisfied that she was alone, she walked further into the churchyard. Her boots crunched on the gravel path as she headed to a secluded wooden bench beneath the gnarled branches of a towering yew tree.

This graveyard was one of her favourite places to rest after an exploration. It was a quiet sanctuary where she could gather her thoughts and write her notes while the impressions were still fresh. It was a kind of staging area between her life beneath, where time slowed and she lost herself in subterranean wonder, and the real world, where she had to conform once more to other people's expectations.

Max reached the bench and put down her pack, then brushed her hands over her worn cargo trousers to dislodge some of the stone dust and grit.

Her black skin was smudged with the remnants of her expedition. She was exhausted, but her dark eyes sparkled, a stark contrast to her professional demeanour during her day job at the water board. Her unruly hair, a cascade of tight curls, was pulled back into a practical low ponytail, highlighting the sharp angles of her features.

She bore the marks of adventure on her body, which she considered an acceptable price to pay for the privilege of venturing off the beaten path.

The most prominent was a jagged scar that snaked its way across her forearm, a stark reminder of misjudged footing in a crumbling factory. Max had plunged through a rotted wooden floor and caught her arm on a shard of rusted metal. It was a deep wound and hard to explain in the emergency room, but the experience had only heightened her appreciation for the perilous beauty of the world she explored so often alone.

Once she had exhausted the derelict places and abandoned structures above ground, Max had started exploring the underground catacomb beneath Edinburgh. It had been several years now, and she still had so much to explore — and so many questions to answer.

She sat down on the bench, pulled out an energy bar, and wolfed it down before retrieving a battered spiral notebook from her pack. Max flicked it open to reveal a myriad of hand-drawn maps.

Each line was a record of her exploration of the hidden passages, forgotten tunnels, and underground arteries of the ancient city. Taking out a pencil, Max updated one specific area of the map. She had revisited it tonight in order to improve the detail of her layout, which later she would transfer to her computer.

She frowned, her brow furrowing in concentration as she marked several side tunnels with tiny question marks for investigation another night.

To Max, urban exploration — urbex — was far more than just a hobby or a daring pastime that skirted the edges of illegality. It was freedom from the confines of surface norms, those rules followed by people at home in the cornered, structured city. Her parents were among those who followed all the rules. They were second-generation Senegalese immigrants who worked hard to prove they belonged here. But Max had never been to Africa. She was Scottish through and through and she loved her home city. There was just something about the way it had been sanitised for tourists that set her teeth on edge, especially in the summer during the festival — and it was down in the dark, silent, and often forgotten places that Max found her sanctuary.

The world above had become a sterile, predictable landscape of comfort and conformity. A place of plush armchairs, pastel-coloured walls, and the constant hum of espresso machines churning out frothy, sugary concoctions. The city had been tamed and domesticated, stripped of its wild unpredictability, leaving its inhabitants cocooned in a bubble of mediocrity. Max had to live in it and work enough to eat and pay rent, but she found every opportunity to escape below ground.

Venturing into the hidden spaces beneath was a way to reclaim the raw essence of existence, to break free from the monotony of modern life and rediscover the sense of adventure that had been all but extinguished for most. Down in the abandoned tunnels and forgotten ruins, Max found a world teetering on the edge of danger, where the unknown lurked around every corner.

Each underground tunnel, every eerie echo, and even the

chill of the damp earth: They all spoke to her, whispering stories of a primitive history where humanity lived closer to the awareness of mortality. This too shall pass.

But there was more to these tunnels than the long dead.

Something lived in the catacomb.

Something with a guttural roar that echoed through the labyrinth of stone. Something that lived within a section of the underneath ringed by symbols of power.

Max was determined to map the extent of the symbols so that other urbexers would be safe in their exploration. Night after night she descended, the dark shadows under her eyes testament to her lack of sleep and singular purpose.

But she drove herself on.

She couldn't bear to lose anyone else.

CHAPTER 7

It had been a chill night last winter as Max and Naomi, another experienced urbexer, had ventured into a new section of the catacomb. Naomi, with her audacious grin and sparkling eyes, had always been the more daring one, and that night they pushed deeper than Max had adventured before.

At the end of a wide tunnel, they found a smaller tunnel branching off at a steep angle. A strange symbol was carved into the rock above it — a monstrous rendition of a Celtic triskelion, each of the three spiralling arms ending in a demonic head with sharp teeth in jaws opened wide.

Any mention of the symbols or rumour of what they might protect had been quashed by the city, and pictures mysteriously disappeared from public websites and social media. Official city tours stayed in the safer areas of the catacomb, patrolled by guards with weapons that seemed out of proportion to the dangers of the world beneath.

But the symbols were a challenge for the urbexer community.

Some had dared venture beyond them, returning with photos and evidence of more ancient tunnels below. Others had emerged with pale faces and wide eyes, with tales of horror glimpsed in the shadows. Most of those gave up urbexing altogether.

A few explorers had never returned to the surface. There were rumours of deep crevasses they might have fallen in, and tales of a monstrous roar that shook even the thickest rock walls to a hail of dust.

While Max had sometimes felt a desire to push deeper into the catacomb, there were more than enough places to find the edge she sought outside of the ring of symbols.

But that night, Naomi walked up to the tunnel entrance and traced the lines of the triskelion with a fingertip. "We should at least go a little way in. Just imagine what we might find."

She turned around, her eyes shining with curiosity. "Whatever once lived down here must be gone by now. Listen, it's quiet."

She tilted her head to one side and Max held her breath as they listened together.

The drip of water on stone, the skitter of insects, and the subtle whisper of a draft of air.

But under the normal sounds of the underworld, deeper in the tunnel, Max thought she could hear the rasp of something sharp on stone.

She shook her head. "I'm not going in. We have a plan for the exploration tonight. Let's just stick to it."

"Oh, come on. Live a little."

With a shrug and a teasing smile, Naomi plunged into the shadows, her figure swallowed by the enveloping darkness.

The last thing Max saw was the patch sewn on Naomi's backpack. A raised fist with middle finger extended, the logo of her favourite band and symbolic of her attitude to the establishment above ground.

Max stood with her hands braced on either side of the tunnel entrance.

Part of her wanted to go on, explore alongside her friend and discover what wonders lay below. There must be a hidden mystery, a treasure worth protecting down there. Maybe it was worth the risk.

But something in the darkness made the hair rise on the back of her neck and her heart thud harder in her chest. Something in the carved stone triskelion and the rumours of horrors below kept her from stepping inside.

"Come on, Max. You have to see this!" Naomi's voice came from the tunnel ahead.

Max took a step inside the tunnel.

There was a sudden ricochet of stones falling as if Naomi had dislodged something.

A desperate scrabbling — then silence, a stillness that hung heavy and foreboding in the air.

Naomi's scream echoed through the tunnel, followed by a guttural roar from the throat of something huge and powerful.

The scream was cut short.

Max froze, paralysed with fear.

Another roar, closer this time.

She turned and ran, back up toward the light, back into the safety of the world above.

Two hours later, Max stood across the road from a police station, her gaze fixed on the grey, imposing structure. She had to tell them what happened, to confess she had left her friend behind. They would surely send a team back into the depths of the catacomb to find Naomi.

But the law was clear. Urbexing skirted the edge of illegality, and the city authorities had issued many stern warnings about the dangers lurking in the underbelly of Edinburgh. There was no question that going beyond the symbols was forbidden.

Max's mind raced as she contemplated her options. She should go inside, report Naomi's disappearance, and face the consequences of her actions.

But the thought of what might follow stopped her from crossing the road.

She could be arrested, her hard-fought life overturned in

an instant. She had clawed her way out of poverty, securing a small flat and a basic day job that provided for her needs.

The thought of losing it all was unbearable.

But it was not just the potential loss of physical comfort that held her back. It was the freedom she cherished, the liberty she found in the silent, forgotten places of the city. Urbexing was her escape, her solace, her rebellion against the strictures of the world. It gave her a sense of control she couldn't find anywhere else. The prospect of being confined, of being caged like an animal, was terrifying.

In her heart, Max knew Naomi was lost to whatever horror lived in the depths of the catacomb. There was no point in them both losing a life.

She walked away and later phoned in an anonymous tip. No one came asking. No one questioned her about Naomi's disappearance.

As the days passed, Max's guilt ate away at her. She found herself down in the catacomb every night, driven to make up for her cowardice. When she did sleep, Max woke in a pool of sweat, her mind echoing with Naomi's scream and the guttural roar of an invisible monster.

Her mission now was clear: to map the entire catacomb, every twisting tunnel, every treacherous turn, and every blind corner that held unseen danger, recording the locations of the triskelion symbols that bounded the path to a darker underworld.

Max uploaded every detail and every discovery onto the Edinburgh urbexer server. She had a debt to pay and she would make things right, one inch of the map at a time.

Once she had updated her notebook, Max left the graveyard and walked back to her modest council flat in Muirhouse. The building was an old, weathered tenement, its once vibrant red bricks now a dull terracotta hue.

It was always difficult to transition between the two sides of her life, especially when she felt so much more alive underground.

Max fumbled with her keys before opening the door to the cramped living space, the smell of damp and mould greeting her as she stepped inside.

The walls were plastered with intricate plans of the catacomb beneath the city, and hand-drawn maps stretched across every available surface. Tattered architectural blueprints, old newspaper articles, and grainy photographs added to the chaotic collage that dominated the room. A web of red strings joined the places where the symbols marked the tunnels, with only parts of the puzzle left to be mapped.

In one corner of the room, a single bed lay unmade, its sheets tangled and pillows askew. A small, cluttered desk was pushed against the opposite wall, its surface buried beneath piles of notebooks, pens, and research materials.

Max sat at the desk and powered on her old, battered laptop, its fan whirring loudly as it struggled to life.

She logged onto a VPN to hide her location, then opened Hidden Depths, the private Discord server she managed, dedicated to urbexing Edinburgh.

Hidden Depths was a tight-knit community of like-minded individuals who shared a passion for discovering the city's forgotten secrets. They were loners who occasionally explored together. They also shared photographs and stories on the forum, exchanging tips and information about the city's uncharted territories.

The images they captured served not only to document the haunting beauty of these abandoned spaces, but also to immortalise fleeting moments, which would otherwise disappear into the abyss of time, unacknowledged and forgotten.

Urbexers considered them a glimpse into a potential future where nature had reclaimed what was once the domain of humanity — a *memento mori*, a reminder of the impermanence of life against the inexorable march of time. Max was strangely comforted by the thought that nothing would remain of us.

She uploaded her latest map additions and photos, as well as detailed renderings of the tunnel she had explored that night.

A flurry of notifications appeared, signalling new messages and reactions to her previous posts.

Max scrolled through the chat, her eyes scanning the messages for any useful tidbits or fresh perspectives.

A lively discussion had emerged about the possible origins of the triskelion symbol. Some members suggested ties to ancient Celtic mythology, while others leaned toward a more sinister explanation involving a secret society and a hidden ritual performed by the elite who ruled the city.

One member had posted a new photo, an ancient archway carved with the symbol of the catacomb, crawling with the strange lichen that thrived in the underneath.

Max felt a prickle down her spine as she looked into the darkness beyond.

She was sure there was something down there, waiting. Hungry.

CHAPTER 8

The city pulsated with the vibrant rhythm of the festival as Walker weaved through the energetic crowd, a solitary figure amidst a sea of revelry.

Music from various entertainment stages joined in a discordant symphony — the bass throb of a rock band, the buoyant strains of a folk fiddler, and the ever-present drone of bagpipes. The scent of food stalls wafted through the air with the sizzle of hog roast, fried chips and gravy, and a tang of Thai spice.

The glow of a massive bonfire spilled over in the street ahead. Its soaring flames cast grotesque, flickering shadows onto the gathered crowd, the spirit of the festival embodied in the dancing figures encircling the inferno.

As he passed, Walker thought he saw monstrous figures writhing and twisting within the heart of the blaze. Their grotesque forms were distorted by the dance of flame as they clawed their way out from the glowing embers.

The vision sent Walker hurtling back into the past as the memory of the burning tomb assaulted him.

The roar of fire. The screams of his dying team. Flames licking at his skin as the intense heat seared his flesh. He was trapped, the exit blocked, the tomb an inferno.

Walker shook his head, a silent attempt to dispel the

haunting memories. He hurried away, skirting the edge of the crowd to find a quieter area.

The sudden vibration of his phone in his pocket jolted Walker from his grim reverie.

He pulled it out and frowned at the unfamiliar number on the screen before answering.

"Hello, is that Emily's dad?" The woman's tone was urgent.

A cold bolt of fear shot through Walker, his heart pounding. "Yes, is she alright? Who is this?"

"I'm Laurel. I found her locket with your number in the park."

Relief flooded over Walker, washing away the icy dread. Emily must have mislaid it while she was out with Tom. Perhaps she hadn't even noticed it was missing.

"Oh right, I'm sure she just dropped it," he replied, his voice steady now. "I can meet you and collect it tomorrow if that's okay."

"No, you don't understand. It's urgent. She's in danger. I saw her pushed into a van. But I can't go to the police. I… heard something. It's important. Can we meet so I can explain?"

Walker's mind whirled, trying to process the sudden influx of information. A surge of adrenalin coursed through him.

"Where are you?"

"I'm in the park still, but I can be at the Scott Monument within ten minutes. Do you know it?"

"Yes, I'm on my way."

As he ended the call and checked the map on his phone, Walker slipped into military mode, his movements automatic even as his mind swirled with questions.

He hurried through the crowd toward the Scott Monument, a looming gothic spire that pierced the night sky. Its blackened arches were stained with the soot of the ancient city, from the coal and peat smoke that had hung over Edinburgh in a thick fog.

As Walker drew closer, he saw a solitary figure standing at its base, her flame-red hair contrasting vividly with the darkened stone. She wore black, and even from a distance, he could discern the bold tattoos etched on her arms, an intricate tapestry of mythological symbols. There was an air of quiet intensity about her.

As Walker approached, he called out. "Laurel?"

She turned, her striking features etched with concern, her green eyes holding a depth that suggested she was no stranger to the darker aspects of life.

"Yes. You're Emily's dad?"

He nodded. "I'm Walker Kane. What happened? What did you see?"

Laurel held out the golden locket, the engraved jewellery glinting in the faint glow of nearby street lamps. "I found this in the park."

Walker took the locket, gripping it tightly as Laurel recounted what she had witnessed. Tom forcing Emily into a van, the hidden chamber in the library — and the chilling words the chancellor had spoken of a sacrifice.

It sounded insane, but Laurel didn't seem to be unhinged as she showed him pictures on her phone to back up her account.

Once she finished, Walker pulled out his phone and called Emily's number.

It rang through to voicemail, which was what he would have expected on a night like this, anyway.

He tried again, and it rang out once more.

He wanted to dismiss Laurel's story as some kind of conspiracy theory, but why would she lie? Something about the situation made him deeply concerned for Emily. Even if she hadn't been kidnapped by some powerful hidden group, he wanted to be sure she was safe.

"Let's go find this chancellor then. You said he's speaking at the festival tonight?"

Laurel shook her head. "We can't just waltz into a black-tie event and demand to speak to him. The chancellor is not just influential. He's formidable. This so-called Cabal clearly controls the city, the police, everything. If we go to the authorities, we'll be ensnared in a web of bureaucracy and denial while Emily..." Her voice trailed off, the implication clear.

Laurel pulled out a small antique book from her backpack.

She paged through until she came to a detailed map. It showed a labyrinth of tunnels and chambers, with sections marked with strange symbols and illustrations of macabre creatures.

"I think they've taken Emily here to the Chamber of Offering." She pointed to a location deep within the catacomb.

Walker assessed the map. While it wasn't the precise and detailed information he was used to on a search and rescue mission, it looked like it would be possible to navigate the depths.

Laurel looked at her watch. "We still have time to reach her before the time of the sacrifice."

"We?"

"You can't go alone. You don't know Edinburgh at all." Her gaze was resolute. "The Cabal has ruled unchecked for too long. I can't stand by and do nothing when I have the chance to make a difference. Let me help you find Emily."

Walker considered his options, then nodded. It would be faster to at least get started with some help. He could slip away from her later if she started to slow him down.

Laurel pulled out her phone, the glow of the screen illuminating her pale face. "We need someone familiar with the catacomb, someone who can help us navigate underground quickly, and I think I know where we can find them."

She swiped, clicked, and then turned the screen toward him.

The image showed a detailed carving, an intricate and unsettling Celtic triskelion with a trio of spiralling arms intertwined with grotesque depictions of monstrous heads.

"It's a marker, a signpost of sorts pointing the way to the heart of the catacomb."

"Where did you find this?"

"It was on a mural in the hidden chapel where I overheard the chancellor's plans, and images like this have been posted on an urbex site. Urban exploration is mostly illegal infiltration, like going into abandoned buildings, old tunnels, anywhere off-limits. But this image was posted by a user named Tenebris219 on Hidden Depths, an urbex community forum. They're online right now."

Laurel started typing again, her fingers tapping out a message to the anonymous urbexer. "We're going to need their help if we're going to reach Emily in time."

CHAPTER 9

As Max scanned the new posts on the Hidden Depths forum, a private message notification popped up.

It was from a new user, Red324.

> Urgent. Help needed.

Intrigued, Max clicked on it and skimmed over the text.

As she read the words, her heart pounded in her chest, her casual interest rapidly replaced with unease. The message detailed a potential abduction, a young woman in danger, and a plea for help.

But it was the reference to the catacomb and the symbol that truly caught her attention. Whoever this was, they wanted to go beyond the symbol, down into the lower depths of the catacomb.

She typed a response. A single word:

> No.

She couldn't go back there, not after what happened. She was playing her part by helping people avoid danger, not run headlong into it.

Her finger hovered over the Send button, ready to shut the door on Red324's plea.

But then, Naomi's face flashed in her mind's eye.

She had charged ahead, fearless and full of life, only to be swallowed by the darkness.

The guilt that had hounded Max since that night rose up.

She stared at the screen.

Perhaps this was a chance to make amends. Perhaps she could help save this young woman, where she hadn't been able to save Naomi.

Her hand shook as she deleted her response, leaving her staring at the empty text box.

Max pushed her chair back and stood up, pacing the confines of her flat, looking around at the maps that papered the walls.

Who was she kidding? Her entire purpose right now was driven by what lay below. She had to help. She couldn't let another young woman disappear into the catacomb. She owed it to Naomi to do this.

Max leaned over the desk, her fingers dancing over the keys.

Meet me by All Saints churchyard in 30 mins.

With a swift click, she sent the message off to Red324, her heart pounding in her chest.

This was real. She was committed.

Immediately, Max set to work, grabbing her worn urbex pack from the corner of the room. It had seen better days, the once vibrant fabric faded and stained, but it was a trusted companion, especially on her solo expeditions. She unzipped it to check the gear inside.

A sturdy rope, a compact first aid kit, and a Leatherman multi-tool. A headlamp, separate hand torch, and spare batteries. A pair of heavy-duty gloves, a dust mask, a small digital camera, and finally, her battered notebook and pen, ready for the next update.

She dug out a few bars of Kendal Mint Cake from her stash under the bed — the slab of sugar was her energy booster of choice — then zipped up her bag and slung it over her shoulder, heading back out into the dark.

After a dash through the city streets, Max arrived at the back of the churchyard. She stood in the shadows of some high-rise council flats as she observed the two figures waiting for her.

Caution was critical, as the police had arrested other urbexers after drawing them out in forums. She needed to be sure that these people were genuinely seeking her help and not setting her up.

The man stood with an alert stance, his military bearing clear in the way he held himself. He was mid-forties and had a couple of days of stubble on his face. His eyes held a haunted look, as if he had seen things he couldn't forget. But despite the weariness in his gaze, he scanned the area with practiced vigilance, keenly aware of his surroundings.

The younger woman accompanying him was angular in appearance, her face devoid of makeup and beautiful in its stark simplicity. Her dyed red hair was tied back in a tight ponytail, a striking contrast against her pale skin, and Max could see intricate tattoos on her arms.

Her elfin figure suggested she wasn't cut out for anything too strenuous. But as the light caught her eyes, Max thought perhaps the woman had a core of steel that might sustain her. It might not be for long as they both had small day packs, and neither was dressed appropriately to go underground. They looked as if they had just walked out of the festival with nothing more than an urgent need to get into the catacomb.

But the underneath tested all, and Max was willing to see how far these two would go.

"Red324?" she asked, as she stepped out of the shadows.

The woman nodded. "Yes, I'm Laurel. This is Walker — he's the father of the missing young woman, Emily."

Walker gazed intently at Max, clearly assessing her. "I'm ex-military Search and Rescue. If you can get me down to the catacomb entrance and help me out with some gear, I can find my daughter. You won't need to stay down there long."

He evidently didn't have a clue what was down there, but Max just nodded at his clear urgency. "I'm Max. I can take you to a tunnel that leads to the depths. Then we can decide on the next step. Do you at least have some warm clothes and torches?"

They both nodded.

"Then follow me."

Max led Walker and Laurel through the dark trees at the back of the churchyard. They walked behind a fence at the back of the property, then along a winding, narrow path between rows of houses.

A little further on, hidden in the shadows, a seemingly forgotten access hole cover lay half-concealed by creeping tendrils of ivy that had claimed it as their own.

Max carefully pulled the ivy away, revealing corroded metal beneath. "I haven't used this entrance in a while, but it'll get us deeper into the catacombs more quickly."

Walker helped her pry open the access hole cover, moving deliberately to avoid the grating sound of metal against metal. They laid it carefully to one side.

An abyss of darkness yawned below, and a dank smell wafted up from the depths.

Max leaned over and listened to the void, closing her eyes so she could concentrate. She could hear the distant drip of water and the faint scurrying of unseen creatures. Under it all, the almost imperceptible hum of the city, muffled by layers of earth that separated the world of the living from the hidden depths.

But there was nothing out of the ordinary.

"I'll go down first. Laurel, you follow next, and Walker, can you pull the cover back over after we descend?"

He nodded.

Max turned on her head torch and began her descent into the darkness, gripping the cold, slippery rungs of the ladder as she wondered what the hell she was doing. It was irresponsible to bring two strangers down here. She might be putting them all in danger.

But the memory of Naomi's final, silenced scream drew her on.

She continued to descend until she stood at the bottom and waited for Laurel and Walker to join her.

Once they reached the bottom of the ladder, Max stared into the tunnel beyond, her head torch illuminating the abandoned passageway that stretched out before them. The walls were made of stone, worn smooth by the passage of time and years of flooding.

"This tunnel used to be an access point for the sewers, abandoned after the construction of the modern city network. It still floods in heavy storms, but we should be fine tonight."

She turned to Walker and Laurel. "I'll take you further in, but I have some rules for safety. Stay together and maintain visual contact. It's easy to get disoriented down here. If you find yourself alone, stay still and call out. I'll come back for you."

She pointed at the worn, uneven stones under their feet. "Be careful where you step. The ground can be slippery with hidden holes or weak spots. If you feel lightheaded, dizzy, or have difficulty breathing, let me know immediately. We might be in an area with low oxygen levels or poisonous gases." She grinned. "Fun, right?"

Walker gave a low laugh. "I appreciate your focus on safety, but we have to hurry. Emily is in grave danger. Laurel, show Max where we need to get to on the map."

Laurel pulled off her pack and opened the flap, gently lifting out a book. It had a blackened leather cover and was weathered with age. Something about it seemed to consume the light from their torches, as if its darkness had a kind of gravity.

Laurel opened the book and turned the pages to a map of the catacomb.

Max bent to look more closely at the twisting labyrinth of tunnels and chambers. She recognised sections she had pinned to her walls and others that she had not yet explored.

Each curve and corner was precisely drawn, with thin lines representing narrow paths, while thicker ones indicated larger passages. There were depictions of the underground geographic terrain — rivers, rocks, even a garden — but there were also sketches of disturbing creatures. Each was more grotesque than the last, as if their forms had been drawn with an artist's hand, but a madman's mind.

As Max examined the pages, she swallowed hard, her throat suddenly dry. "I recognise some of these sections. Where do you need to get to?"

Laurel pointed at a particular chamber, far beyond the markings that bounded the safe area. "The Chamber of Offering."

"Can you get us there?" Walker asked.

Max couldn't help but follow the twisting tunnels on the map down to the heart of the catacomb, where a monstrous beast stood in front of a fiery volcanic pit.

Its hulking frame was wreathed in shadow. Its eyes glowed with a malevolent light as it stood with talons raised and jaws agape, ready to devour its prey. A word written in black ink labeled the creature — Grendsluagh.

Was this what had taken Naomi? And how could these two hope to rescue its next victim?

Max considered leaving them right there and climbing the ladder back to the surface. She could forget she had ever met them. At least she would see the dawn that way. It was surely madness to confront whatever prowled the depths.

"Max? Can you get us down there?" Walker said again,

breaking into her thoughts.

She blinked and took a deep breath. "I'll take you as far as this section." She pointed on the map to a fork in the tunnel. "Then you should be able to reach this chamber without me. As you can see, there is a more established tunnel that leads back up to the basement levels of the university from the chamber. You could exit that way without my help."

Walker nodded. "Right, let's go then. We need to hurry."

Max set off at the front of the trio, with Laurel behind and Walker bringing up the rear.

They moved as fast as they could in the narrowing tunnel, careful to avoid the trip hazards, but as they descended, Max couldn't shake the feeling of unease. She normally enjoyed the transition from above to beneath, but this time, the walls closed around her, and there were whispers of dread under the echo of their footfalls. The atmosphere was oppressive as the weight of centuries bore down upon them, suffocating them in its dark promise as they spiralled into the depths.

For the sake of Naomi's memory, she would take Walker and Laurel to the edge of the ring of symbols, but then they would be on their own.

CHAPTER 10

As Walker followed Max and Laurel through the tunnel, he silently urged them to move faster. Those who had taken Emily were at least an hour ahead of them. Even though Laurel had spoken of a timetable for this potential sacrifice, he was desperate to get to his daughter.

He ducked to avoid a low-hanging piece of masonry. It was clear evidence of how unstable this tunnel was, but he trusted this urbexer, Max, to at least get them as far as she dared to go. Walker had recognised fear in her eyes as she looked at the map — not of the catacomb, as she walked with confidence here — but of the creature at its heart.

The Grendsluagh looked terrifying indeed, but it must surely be a myth. Those who kidnapped young women and carried them to an underground cavern usually had base desires, which they shrouded in ritual as an excuse for their depravity. Rumours of the beast would be an effective way to keep prying eyes from their dark acts. Walker clenched his fists as he considered what he would do to any who laid a finger on Emily.

He slowly exhaled to calm his anger and examined the tunnel around him as it continued to slowly spiral down, now at a steeper angle.

Walker was used to working underground, but he usually

had a team with him on a mission, or at least others skilled in navigating and operating in confined and dangerous places. Max was clearly capable, but Laurel seemed at once fragile and as unyielding as the bedrock this tunnel was carved into. Trying to persuade her to give him the ancient book and leave was clearly pointless. But once they reached the fork leading to the Chamber of Offering, he would find a way to ditch them both and continue alone at a faster pace. He didn't want to be responsible for their safety and his only focus was finding Emily.

"Careful up ahead," Max called back. "There's a section that is much worse than the last time I was here. We need to clamber over slowly to stop it sliding."

She helped Laurel through, and Walker climbed with ease after them both.

In the chamber beyond, Max pointed to a collapsed wall in the side of the tunnel. "We enter here to reach the lower levels. Be careful — it's tight. In the cavern below, only step where I step."

Walker crouched down and followed on, and the tunnel soon opened out into a long cave.

It was clearly far older than the modern tunnels above, a relic of pre-industrial times. A weathered stalactite hung from the roof of the cave, its angular pointed tip reminding Walker of the sword of Damocles, as if their fate might hang by a thread.

As he pushed the ominous thought aside, Laurel walked a little closer to examine its unusual shape. "This is depicted on the map, I'm sure of it. We're definitely on the right track."

She took another step forward as she swung her pack around.

"No!" Max shouted. "Get back!"

A rock beneath Laurel's feet shifted as she tried to reverse direction.

A heavy clunking sound of huge hidden gears.

A hail of rocks and debris rained down from the ceiling. Small stones at first — then an enormous boulder smashed into the ground, causing cracks to form around it.

The rumble of something gigantic came from above.

"Run!" Walker shouted.

The ground shook as the rumble grew louder.

Out in front, Max stumbled forward, her arms flailing. She reached out to the wall for support, huddling close to the rock, protecting her head.

"This way!" she called out.

But Laurel was frozen in place near the stalactite, mesmerised as the tiny cracks fractured the surrounding rock, leaving her on a fissured web.

Walker could read the stone as clearly as if it were lightning branches in a stormy sky.

It would collapse, and Laurel would be taken with it into the abyss.

He sprinted toward her as falling rocks glanced off his broad shoulders.

He bent down then sprung up, using all his force to lift and push Laurel — catapulting her to safety just as a fissure opened up across the cavern floor.

The solid rock splintered apart with seismic violence as cracks on either side fanned out.

The ground collapsed under him — Walker fell into the abyss.

CHAPTER 11

As the ground fell away, instinct took over. Walker arched his back, twisting in the air as he grappled for purchase.

The cave spun around him in a wild cyclone of dust and debris.

He reached out, fingers splayed, hoping for something, anything.

Contact — the rough, unforgiving texture of rock. His fingers wrapped around an outcrop, clawing into the stone with desperate strength.

He grabbed on. His body slammed against the hard stone wall, knocking the wind from him as he gasped, lungs straining for air in the gritty, dust-choked cavern.

Above him, the ceiling continued to crumble, showering him with smaller stones.

He shielded his face against his arm, eyes squeezed shut, gritting his teeth against the stinging onslaught of the cave-in. The shower of rocks fell like rain, pinging against his arms and back.

The clamour was deafening in the confined tunnel — until, finally, it eased to a light shower of rock dust and sand.

"Walker!" Laurel shouted from above. "Are you okay?"

Walker looked up, squinting as he blinked away the grit from the cave-in. He was only ten metres or so from the surface edge — but on the opposite side to where he needed to be.

"Just about. Are you and Max alright?"

Laurel gazed down with concern. "Yes, just a bit bruised. I'm so sorry, I must have triggered something."

Max appeared beside her and assessed the scene with an expert gaze. "It doesn't matter now. We just need to get out of here. The cave isn't stable."

"No kidding," Walker said to himself as he glanced down to search for a foothold.

The chasm gaped beneath him, with the faint, hollow echoes of fallen debris betraying its depth.

Walker swallowed hard as memories of his search and rescue days flooded back. Images of bodies dashed on jagged rocks, soft flesh broken apart by hard stone and gravity. The lucky ones were dead, for those who survived lay in agony with shattered bones, crippled and helpless in the dark.

He might not die if he fell. He knew that much. But Emily... Emily might as well be dead if he did.

With a deep, ragged inhale, Walker shifted his gaze back upwards to assess the route out. Sweat stung his eyes, mixing with the grime and dust from the cave-in. He blinked it away.

The broken rock wall was craggy and uneven, with enough possibilities for him to climb.

He tentatively swung his right leg beneath him, toes probing for something solid. His boot scraped against rough, uneven stone, sending a tiny avalanche of pebbles spiralling into the abyss as he found purchase on a jutting outcrop.

Walker pressed his weight onto the ledge, his body tensing in anticipation of a possible slip.

But the rock held firm.

He began to climb, muscles tense as his fingertips probed the crevices in the rock, seeking even the shallowest of holds.

Suddenly, his boot skidded, the smooth stone beneath offering no grip.

He clenched his fingers tighter, the sharp edges of the rock biting into his skin until he found a new hold.

Walker clung to the rock for a moment, as the chill of a near miss ran down his spine.

"Not much further," Max shouted. "Just a few more metres. I'm going to rig up a rope to help you across to this side once you get to the top."

Get to the top. Her words echoed in Walker's mind as he reached up and found another hold, levering himself up one painstaking inch at a time.

Finally, after what seemed an age, Walker hauled himself up over the lip of the crevasse and lay panting on the edge. His chest heaved as each ragged breath clawed its way in and out of his lungs.

He closed his eyes for a moment, calming his breathing. He had to dampen the surge of adrenalin and gather his energy for what must come next.

He had to cross the chasm.

After his breathing returned to normal, Walker rolled to his knees and stood up, assessing the situation.

Laurel stood on the other side, her black clothes now mottled grey with rock dust. Her face was pale and drawn, the stark lines of worry evident even in the dim light of her torch.

Max stood by the wall of the cavern, holding a coil of rope, her posture capable and assured.

She gestured at a rough route across the wall.

"That looks like the best way. I think the rope is long enough. I'll throw it across. Rig it on that end for extra support on the way over."

Walker was suddenly grateful to have her along, appreciative of her climbing experience. His muscles quivered, raw from the exertion of the clamber up the cliff. His hands, already bruised and bloodied, ached with a persistent throb. The thought of clinging to the wall once more, inches from falling into the dark abyss, seemed like an impossible challenge right now.

But every minute they were not pushing forward was another minute that Emily was in danger.

"Okay, throw it over," he called out.

Max attached a stone to the end of the rope as a weight and, with a powerful arc of her arm, she launched it across to Walker with practiced ease.

The rope uncoiled in mid-air and landed with a thud at his feet, stirring up a cloud of rock dust as Max anchored her end securely.

As Walker bent to pick it up, he glanced over the edge.

In the depths of the chasm, his head torch glinted off something white, something moving far below.

Something climbing toward him.

Walker frowned, trying to see what it was, but his torch wasn't strong enough. "Max, shine your light down there, will you?"

Max walked to the edge and looked down so her head torch joined his in lighting up the deeper strata of the abyss.

"What the hell?" Walker gasped as the creature climbed into the dim light.

A giant spider scaled the chasm wall, its form a mutated fusion of the living and the dead, constructed from a charnel mosaic of bones. They gleamed with an ethereal pallor, each one a remnant of a long-forgotten victim, like an ossuary brought to unholy life.

Its eyes were a chilling void, empty sockets staring ahead with a blank, sightless gaze. Its mandibles snapped open and shut as it climbed, its jaws resembling ancient sickles, with sharp serrated edges. As it moved, its bony legs clicked and clacked against the rock.

Walker calculated the time it would take for the spider to reach the top at its glacial pace. If he hurried, he would make it over with more than enough time to avoid it.

He picked up the end of the rope.

As he turned to anchor it, his boot knocked against a couple of small stones. They tumbled over the edge, clattering against the rock before disappearing into the abyss.

"Hurry, Walker!" Laurel shouted.

At the urgency in her voice, Walker turned back to look down once more down into the abyss.

The spider had quickened its climb.

And it was not alone.

CHAPTER 12

Alerted by the clatter of falling stones, more of the nightmare creatures boiled out of the darkened cracks and crevices of the deeper catacomb.

They surged like a wave up the side of the fissure, skeletal forms skittering up the stone, their clacking jaws creating an ominous chorus that echoed in the chamber.

Walker was out of time.

He spun around. With precision honed from years in search and rescue, he swiftly secured the rope to the boulder, careful to anchor it high enough to offer a vital handhold during his precarious crossing.

He tested the knot by applying his weight. The rope held firm.

Turning back to the abyss, Walker sized up his path across the cavern wall. A few feet away, a narrow ledge jutted out, an unsteady path hanging precariously over the chasm.

It was treacherous. One wrong move could send him plunging down into the waiting jaws of those skeletal nightmares.

Taking a deep breath, he carefully manoeuvred his way toward the ledge, his heart pounding in his chest.

The stones under his feet were unstable, shifting and groaning beneath his weight. He had to move slowly, cautiously.

But the scraping of bone against rock came from below, with the eerie clack of the spiders' jaws. They were so close.

He had to hurry.

As Max and Laurel urged him on from the far side, Walker traversed the treacherous rock face step by step.

He used the cavern wall as a support and the rope to brace himself with trembling fingers, his muscles twitching with fatigue.

Halfway across, Walker couldn't help but glance down.

The lead spider had narrowed the gap, its skeletal form now a mere few metres away, with the mass of others not far behind.

His muscles were already strained beyond their limits, but with every ounce of strength he had left, Walker made a final, desperate lunge.

He hurled himself across the last section toward the other side.

His fingers brushed Max's outstretched hand, but he fell short, plunging back toward the yawning maw of the chasm, his fingers scrabbling in a futile attempt to find purchase on the unforgiving stone.

Max and Laurel grabbed his arms, desperately pulling him up — just as the bony leg of the first spider touched Walker's leg from below.

He kicked out in horror and revulsion, a hollow clatter echoing through the cavern as his boot connected with the skeletal creature.

The spider tumbled away into the abyss and disappeared into darkness.

But more were already crawling up Walker's body, their sharp bony legs digging into his flesh like tiny knives. Others surged behind and the cavern echoed with a chorus of clicking bone jaws and the clacking of legs against stone.

The sound seemed to reverberate deep inside Walker. He could feel them, a grotesque tide of skeletal bodies crawling up his legs, their bony carapaces clambering over his skin, ready to devour his flesh. He twisted in revulsion, trying to shrug them off, teeth clenched as he suppressed a primal scream.

Above him, Max's grip was unyielding, her fingers locked around his wrist. She hauled him up with every ounce of her strength, her muscles straining as she helped Walker back over the edge.

As he rolled onto solid ground, panting with the effort, the spider horde surged over the edge after him.

Laurel stood her ground. She kicked the creatures, knocking them back, each impact sending more of the nightmares skittering into the inky darkness.

"Run!" Max pointed to a thin, shadowy opening at the far end of the cavern. "Get in the tunnel ahead!"

Laurel raced for the way out, Max and Walker right behind, kicking up clouds of dust in their frantic retreat.

As they ducked into the tunnel, more of the spiders surged over the edge of the abyss and scuttled toward them.

Max was the first to reach the tunnel. "Get more rocks!"

Her hands, scraped and smeared with grime, were a blur of desperate activity as she sought every loose stone, every fragment of rock within her grasp, their rough surfaces catching against her torn skin.

Walker and Laurel joined in, hoisting rocks, panting as their muscles strained with the weight. Each rock they added to the makeshift barricade held more of the nightmares back.

One scuttled over the top.

Laurel was quick to react. She grabbed a hefty stone and smashed it down on the creature. Its bones fractured beneath the impact as a morbid rain of fragments skittered across the cavern floor.

Max shoved the last stone into place and the three of them collapsed against the walls of the tunnel with ragged breaths and aching limbs.

After a moment, Laurel pulled the ancient book out of her pack. "Now we know there are traps in the catacomb, we need to pay more attention to the map." She opened it to a page and pointed out the spiders etched on the edges of the illustration. "I guess we just met these."

"What's next?" Max asked, as she gazed back at the walled-up tunnel with hollow eyes.

Her way home was blocked, and Walker wondered if she regretted her decision to help. But whatever her doubts, he was grateful for Max's expertise. Without her, he would have been food for the spiders and Emily sacrificed to the Grendsluagh without a chance of escape. They might need each other again in the catacomb ahead.

Laurel traced an intricate etching on the map, leaning closer to examine its detail, then she looked up, her eyes wide with horror.

CHAPTER 13

Laurel pointed down at a pool of blue ink in shades from turquoise to midnight showing a gradation of depth. In the middle, a taloned tentacle unfurled sinuously out of the water to snatch at the air.

Max looked over at the image. "Well, at least we know what to expect."

Her words were flippant, but her heart drummed a relentless tattoo against her ribcage. As she tucked a loose curl of hair behind her ear, her fingers trembled. She hid them quickly, not wanting the others to see her response.

The skeletal spiders had been too close. Max suppressed a shudder as she thought of what could have happened.

She should have kept a better eye on Laurel.

She should have kept them all safe.

After Naomi, she couldn't bear the thought of losing someone else under her protection.

She glanced sideways at the map again, her breath catching at the thought of that deep blue water and what hid in its depths. A knot tightened in her stomach.

Max was no stranger to the thrill of adrenalin and the allure of the unknown. As an urbexer, she had faced dark, forgotten tunnels, crumbling structures, and the remnants of human life left untouched for decades. She had stood unflinching at the edge of a decaying building, climbed heights that would make most dizzy, and descended into the city's hidden depths. The adrenalin rush, the challenge of the unexplored, the treasure trove of hidden histories waiting to be unveiled — they all called to her.

But deep water was a different matter entirely.

Max clenched her fists at the chill of memory. She'd stumbled upon a brackish swimming pool in the tangled depths of an abandoned estate and, in the ferocity of a sudden rainstorm, she had slipped and smacked her head. She tumbled into the water, becoming entangled with weeds as she sank into the depths. Her desperate gasps for air only resulted in lungs full of water, the world fading as darkness claimed her.

That day, she had been lucky. She had somehow survived, but the incident had left her with a deep-seated fear that she found hard to control.

Max took a slow breath and placed her hand on the stone floor, anchoring herself to this place and this time. Perhaps if the way behind had still been open, she might have left Walker and Laurel and fled back to the surface.

But the way back was blocked. She had to go on.

Walker stood and brushed the dust from his clothes, stretched his limbs, and rolled his shoulders. Max knew how hard it would have been to make that climb and then the crossing, and he must be in pain after the exertions of his scramble to safety.

"Are you ready?" he asked.

Max pushed herself up from the wall. "As I'll ever be."

Laurel stuffed the book back into her bag as she gave a half smile of apology. "I'll try not to set off any more traps, but let's keep checking the map to be sure we're on the right track."

Max took the lead again, and soon the stone tunnel narrowed even further. They had to crouch over to walk as the dank stone walls pressed closer.

As they walked on, the air became dense. Each breath Max drew felt like inhaling a viscous sludge that clogged her throat. A rancid scent permeated the stagnant air — not the clean salt of the open sea or the fresh green of seaweed, but something dark and grim. The smell of dying things, of forgotten caves and stagnant tidal pools, filled with the corpses of rotting sea creatures.

They rounded a tight bend, and the tunnel opened abruptly, the cramped confines giving way to a vast chamber. The walls stretched out into the distance, too far for their torchlight to reach, disappearing into an all-consuming darkness. The cavern was a monument to geological time, a cathedral of stalactites and stalagmites that dwarfed their human presence.

They stood on a ledge that overlooked the water, the drop steep and unforgiving. A vast subterranean lake spread out before them, its inky surface still and undisturbed.

The sound of waves lapped against a shoreline just out of sight on the other side. A drip-drip-drip of water came from the cavern's ceiling, and there was an occasional splash as something moved beneath the surface.

But between these sounds was an oppressive, heavy silence that seemed to hold the echo of screams long since faded.

Walker raised his torch, the light piercing the oppressive darkness and reflecting off the still surface of the lake.

Shadows shifted beneath the water. The shapes moved just below the surface, leaving behind ripples that danced and twisted in the faltering torchlight.

Something broke the surface.

A ripple, then a splash.

A momentary glimpse of something... other. Was it a fin, or perhaps a tentacle?

The sight of it was so fleeting, it was impossible to tell.

Max stepped back from the edge, trying to calm her

pounding heart. Her vision narrowed in the beginning of what she knew was a panic attack. She had to stop it before it overwhelmed her.

"Is there a way around?" she asked Laurel. "Can we look at the map again?"

"Sure." Laurel pulled off her pack and together, they examined the catacomb.

"It looks like we might be able to go this way," Laurel murmured as she traced a thin line that snaked away from the lake and then around.

It was a longer route, but clearly safer.

Max nodded. "That looks better. The entrance must be around here somewhere."

They searched the area, their torches casting long shadows that danced across the cavern. Max searched every inch of the walls, determined to find another route out of here. There was no way she was going anywhere near that lake.

"Here," Walker called out after a few minutes, but his tone was downcast.

Max and Laurel joined him by a side tunnel — or at least, what was left of it. The entrance was almost completely blocked, filled in with rocks and rubble from subsidence, erosion, and the passage of time.

Max examined the blocked passage, pushing against the rocks. She clambered up the pile to scout a possible way ahead, but she could see no clear way of getting through. Her heart sank.

"Maybe we can clear this?" But even to her own ears, she sounded doubtful.

"We don't have enough time." Walker turned back to face the lake. The silent, sinister body of water now seemed even more daunting. "The only way is across."

He shone his torch back toward the lake. Just beneath the surface of the water were what looked like stepping stones, as if the vertebrae of some ancient leviathan provided a precarious path across the water into darkness.

"We can use those to get across." He walked to the side of the ledge and shone his torch down, Max and Laurel joining him.

The stepping stones were slick with algae, their mossy green surfaces glistening in the torchlight. They seemed to bob slightly with the movement of the water, as though at any moment they might sink beneath, plunging any who dared step on them into the depths below. They were spaced apart, too, some almost too far to comfortably reach.

Max's heart sank at the sight, but their options were limited. She couldn't go back and there was no other option. She had to go on.

Walker shone his torch around as he assessed their options. Finally, he looked up, his torch illuminating the cavernous ceiling high above.

The remnants of a rope bridge hung amongst the shadowed stalactites. Its wooden planks were either missing or hung precariously, and the ropes on either side were torn apart, the ends shredded and ragged. Gashes marred the few remaining planks — deep, jagged grooves that could only have been made by talons and teeth.

"Perhaps we can use that to help us get across."

Max thought it was a long shot, but she would try anything to stay away from that water.

She held her torch steady so Walker could see clearly. He reached up and stretched as far as he could to hook onto a dangling spar, pulling it toward him with a jerk.

It was rotten and crumbled in his hand. Fragments plummeted down, the pieces dropping into the water with a series of splashes, the sound echoing through the cavern like gunshots.

The surface of the water erupted violently, boiling with an unseen creature that attacked the remains of the spar and ripped it apart.

Flashes of silver erupted from the water, illuminated in

the torchlight. Tentacles, sinewy and glistening, reached upwards, slapping against the surface in a frenzy.

Max caught glimpses of wickedly sharp talons, slick with water, and rows of jagged, needle-like teeth that glistened eerily in the light.

CHAPTER 14

As quickly as the frenzy began, it ended.

The water settled back into an ominous calm. The only remnants of the chaos were the ripples that slowly faded away.

Walker turned to Laurel and Max, raising an eyebrow as his gaze met theirs in the dim torchlight. "Guess we need to be careful."

He pointed across to where the stepping stones met the far bank of the lake. "We have to get over there and we have to do it quickly."

To Max, the rough shoreline might as well have been the other end of the world. It lay in shadow, a mere silhouette against the deeper darkness beyond. She needed more time to prepare herself, to psych herself up for the crossing, but Walker wasn't wasting any more precious minutes.

"Let's give it something to keep it occupied while we make a run for it. Get ready."

"No, not yet," Max pleaded, her breath coming fast as the panic threatened.

But Walker reached into his pack and pulled out a knife, its blade glinting ominously in the torchlight.

With a swift motion, he slashed at the remaining ropes of the tattered bridge.

It crashed down into the water next to them, sending up a spray of brackish water that stank of putrid decay and rancid, rotting algae.

The creature beneath the surface attacked the falling bridge, its violent frenzy creating a momentary distraction as the water churned and frothed.

Max stood frozen by the spectacle as the dark waters of traumatic memory threatened to overwhelm her.

"Run!" Walker's sharp command cut through her hesitation as he took off along the stepping stones.

He led the way across the treacherous path, leaping from rock to rock as his head-torch cast long, flickering shadows over the path ahead.

Max forced herself to run after him, her boots slipping on the wet stone as she focused on the next step, and then the next as Laurel followed behind.

The echo of splashing water and the splintering of wood spurred Max on, her fear transforming into raw adrenalin. The far bank of the lake was still an impossible distance away, but she was moving now.

They would make it. She just had to count her steps. Counting helped, and it was only twenty steps to the bank.

Twenty. Nineteen. Eighteen.

Her breath came in sharp gasps as Max lurched from rock to rock, each step a test of balance, a test of will.

Don't look down. Don't look down.

Walker was only a few steps ahead and suddenly he wobbled, his foot slipping sideways on a stone.

He flailed for balance, his torchlight flickering wildly across the water, and the brief moment was enough to break their momentum. Their hurried journey across the stones faltered.

Max paused behind him, her breath coming in ragged gasps.

As Walker regained his balance, there was a moment of silence.

The frenzied splashing behind them had stilled, and the sudden calm sent a chill of foreboding down Max's spine. Her breath hitched in her throat.

Suddenly, something cold and slimy wrapped around her ankle.

She screamed, the sound echoing off the cavern walls.

The grip tightened, sharp spikes digging into her flesh, pulling her off the stepping stone. She thrashed as she tried to break free, but the creature's grip was too strong.

Her head-torch was shaken off and plummeted down into the lake, its spiralling light revealing the monstrous creature lurking below.

A grotesque composition of tentacles and spikes, its translucent body was a horrific array of misshapen forms. As the torchlight glinted off its flesh, it illuminated the creature's inner organs, which glistened and pulsated around some half-digested crustacean, its shell crushed into fragments, its flesh mashed to a pulp.

The gaping maw was like that of a lamprey's, with circular rows of serrated, needle-like teeth surrounded by a whorl of mutated muscle and bone that ground together rhythmically as it drew ever closer.

Max clawed at the slick stepping stone, her nails scraping against the algae-covered surface as the creature dragged her down.

Two more tentacles snaked from the water, wrapping around her arm, tightening, the spikes digging deeper into her flesh.

The slash of a knife.

Walker hacked at its tentacles and the creature convulsed, releasing a black slime that stained the stones and water around them. The dark ichor sizzled in contact with the air, the pungent smell of decay filling the cavern. Its tentacles whipped wildly, spraying droplets of slime that glowed eerily in the dim torchlight.

Laurel grabbed Max's other arm and tugged as Walker continued to attack the creature. Its grip loosened, the tentacles recoiling from the onslaught.

Max was suddenly free. She gasped, her breath coming in ragged pants.

With a grunt of effort, Walker hauled her up out of the water, her sodden weight heavy against his grip. Her breath rasped in her throat as she clung to him, her body trembling with cold and fear.

Together they ran the final few metres, Laurel right behind as they slip-slided across the stepping stones to the far bank.

As soon as her feet touched solid ground, Max fell to her knees. Her legs collapsed with exhaustion and the aftermath of terror, leaving her shivering and shaking.

Laurel crouched by her side. "You're okay now. We made it. You're okay."

A deafening roar echoed through the cavern.

The creature erupted from the depths of the lake, the water parting around its massive form like a tidal wave. Its silhouette was a monstrous shadow, a nightmare painted in a spectrum of darkness.

As it surged upwards, water cascaded from its writhing tentacles, spattering on the rocky bank with the harsh sound of rainfall on stone. Its body oozed sickly black slime from its wounds, the viscous liquid coiling in tendrils through the water like an ink cloud.

It whipped a tentacle toward its prey on the bank, its bulk belying its speed.

Max and Laurel ducked and threw themselves flat against the sharp stones.

The tentacle passed just above them, its wind stirring their hair and carrying the rank stench of the decaying sea dead.

Max and Laurel scrambled to their feet and dashed up

the incline toward Walker at the very edge of the cavern. The ground beneath them was slippery with water and loose, small rocks that crumbled and shifted under their weight, but they pushed as fast as they could to get away from the water.

The creature roared again.

Its tentacles thrashed and thrummed through the water, sending violent waves crashing against the rocky bank. Each monstrous limb rose and fell with a thunderous splash, their talons blindly snatching at the air.

But the creature could not leave the shallows of the water.

At last, it sank back into the depths of the lake, and the waters were still once more.

Max sat on the ground and curled her arms around her legs, shaking with cold and the aftermath of facing the creature. Her clothes clung to her, the fabric heavy and cold against her skin. Her ankle throbbed with pain where the creature had gripped her, the memory of its sharp, slimy tentacles wrapped around her leg still fresh in her mind. She could taste the metallic tang of fear in her mouth and her heart pounded in her chest, a wild drumbeat that echoed in her ears.

Some part of her understood how shock was affecting her, but all Max wanted to do was get out of this nightmare.

She didn't know these people. She didn't want to care about some kidnapped girl, and she certainly did not want to face the monster at the heart of the catacomb. Enough already. The next chance she had, Max was determined to get out and leave them behind.

"Here," Laurel said softly, offering her a warm fleece from her pack. "Take off that wet top and put this on."

Walker turned his back while Max changed, and then he hunkered down next to her, offering her a small bottle of whisky. "I picked this up at the festival earlier this evening. Seems like a long time ago now."

Max took it and gulped down a long draft. The burning liquid certainly helped, and slowly her heart rate returned to normal.

In the cavern's quiet, the lake gently lapped against the shore. The sound was a soothing, rhythmic murmur, a stark contrast to the recent chaos.

For a moment, all was calm.

Then an indistinct sound emanated from the tunnel ahead of them.

It started as a soft, ethereal whisper, barely discernible above the gentle cadence of the water. A spectral hum that meandered through the cavern's dark recesses.

Gradually, the murmur swelled into a more distinct rhythm.

It became a chant, a low dirge that echoed throughout the cavern. The words were an ancient tongue, the language archaic and unrecognisable. It was as though the shadows had found a voice and now summoned the creature that lived at the heart of the catacomb to ascend and take its sacrifice.

Walker stood up, suddenly alert. "Emily." He grabbed his pack and ran into the tunnel, disappearing into the shadows.

CHAPTER 15

Walker raced through the darkened tunnel, his torchlight cutting through the pitch black ahead of him as he followed the rising notes of the chant.

Behind him, he heard running footsteps as Max and Laurel followed.

But he couldn't wait for them.

He had to get to Emily, and something about the eerie chant made him think her time was running out.

His rapid breathing echoed around the stone passage, now covered with unusual lichen and moss. Gnarled roots emerged from the cracked roof above as nature reclaimed its territory.

Walker skidded to a halt as the confining tunnel suddenly opened up into a large circular chamber.

He swept his torchlight across the space.

The room was like the hub of a monstrous wheel, with six tunnels like spokes leading off into darkness. Each entrance was flanked by an arched portal of ancient stone. The chamber walls were covered in intricate carvings, a parade of nightmares immortalised in stone. Twisted creatures with gnashing teeth and gleaming eyes of coloured glass writhed across the walls in a dance of eternal torment.

Walker's torchlight cast the carvings in ghastly relief,

making them appear to writhe and twitch in a semblance of life.

The chant reverberated around the circular chamber, the sound echoing from each of the tunnels. It had become an intertwined symphony of voices that offered no hint of its origin.

Walker dashed to each entrance, straining hard to listen as he tried to work out which way to go. But the acoustics of the chamber twisted and distorted the sound, turning the chant into an omnipresent hum that seemed to come from all directions at once.

There was no time to try every route. He needed Laurel's map.

Walker ran back to the entrance of the tunnel he had emerged from and shouted, "Laurel. Hurry! I need help!"

His words echoed down the passage, but in the distance, he heard her shout in return. "We're coming!"

A few minutes later, Laurel and Max ran out of the tunnel, panting with the effort of running so soon after the ordeal at the lake.

Max sank to the floor, her back against one wall while Laurel bent to pull the book from her pack.

"Which way?" Walker spun around, indicating the various routes as he tried to keep his frustration under control.

He wanted to grab the map from Laurel and continue alone. They were wasting so much time. If this were a well-planned military mission with a trained team, he would have completed it by now. They'd be back on the surface, Emily safe and well and wrapped in an emergency blanket.

But one thing he had learned in the military was the importance of a team, even a makeshift one like this, and he couldn't work out which way to go on his own.

As the eerie chant continued, Laurel placed the book on the ground and turned the pages of the map. "This six-way room is marked, but the map doesn't show the correct route forward. There is a gap between this place and the Chamber of Offering. It must be a test…"

Holding the open book, Laurel began checking the carvings above each archway. "The one we emerged from shows the triple waves for water. This next is a spiral, usually representing life force. Next is an ouroboros, the snake eating its tail." She frowned. "It usually represents the cyclical nature of life, so this could be the one."

She moved onto the subsequent tunnels. "A horn of plenty, for abundance. A bird, perhaps a raven, for wisdom, and a dagger for sacrifice. This should be the most obvious route, but that in itself makes me doubt it."

Laurel spun slowly around once more, assessing them all.

Walker wanted to shake the knowledge from her brain and shout at her to hurry, but he held his tongue.

"The ouroboros." Laurel pointed decisively at the symbol. "It has to be. From what I saw in the library, this sacrifice has been performed for centuries, with each year leading to the next. A never-ending cycle of sacrifice, only to begin afresh each year."

The sounds of chanting suddenly grew louder, the rhythm quickening into something like a call.

A summoning.

They were out of time.

Walker spun around and sprinted toward the ouroboros arch, his boots thudding against the stone floor in a dull echo of the chant.

"Wait!" Laurel shouted from behind, but Walker didn't stop.

He raced under the arch and into the corridor beyond.

After several dogleg turns, the plain stone walls shifted into intricate carvings of grotesque faces and claws. They seemed to reach out toward him as he ran, their monstrous expressions illuminated by the flicker of flaming torches held aloft in iron brackets. At last, a sign they were on the right track. The chamber must be close.

The constricted corridor expanded abruptly, and Walker skidded to a halt. His breathing came in ragged gasps, drowned out by the chanting that was now almost deafening.

A massive circular chamber opened out before him, its dimensions swallowed by shadows that hid its true size.

Towering pillars rose around the circumference of the room, each one sculpted with muscular human figures that bore the weight of the immense ceiling in their upraised hands. Their stone faces were contorted in expressions of struggle and despair.

On the far side of the chamber loomed a colossal boulder with chains crudely hammered into its rough surface. Behind it, the mouth of a dark tunnel yawned, an abyss that swallowed the light.

Twelve robed figures stood in a semicircle around the boulder, swaying rhythmically with the cadence of their chant.

Walker scanned the chamber.

Emily was nowhere in sight. Had she been taken already? Was he too late?

His mind raced as he assessed the scene. Every part of him wanted to run forward, to call out for Emily, to fight these bastards, whoever they were.

But there were twelve of them, and he didn't need military training to know he was outnumbered.

Perhaps Emily wasn't even here.

Walker quietly padded to one side, slipping into the shadows cast by one of the huge pillars. He could now see the space between the robed figures and the boulder.

His heart almost stopped as he saw her.

Emily lay prone just metres away, curled on the stone floor, her slender form dwarfed by the enormity of the massive rock behind her. Her wrists were bound, her eyes closed, but her chest rose and fell rhythmically. She was clearly drugged, but at least she was alive.

A flicker of movement in the tunnel to his left.

Walker turned to see Laurel and Max peering out, their eyes wide as they saw what lay in the chamber. The two women were certainly capable, but Walker couldn't ask them to fight for him or his daughter.

He assessed the options.

He could create a distraction, maybe hurl a rock against the walls or pillars. The loud noise echoing through the chamber might be enough to divert the attention of the hooded figures.

But he dismissed the idea almost as quickly as it had come. They were immersed in their ritual; it would take more than a clatter to draw their attention away from Emily.

Perhaps he could move through the shadows guerrilla-style and take out the robed figures one by one. He certainly relished the prospect of pay-back, but with Emily in such a vulnerable position, there was too much at stake if things went south.

As Walker grappled with the possibilities, Max and Laurel quietly joined him behind the pillar. He was grateful they had chosen to stand with him rather than retreating to safety. Perhaps they would have a chance if they acted together.

A sudden roar broke through the chanting, a guttural bellow that echoed from the yawning mouth of the tunnel beyond the boulder.

It rattled the foundations of the chamber, shaking the dust from the ancient stonework. Walker felt it resonate in his chest, a primal force that made his heart beat faster.

The cadence of the chant changed in response. The ancient language shifted, each word now twisted, echoing with desperation and fear.

It was less a summoning now, more like a plea, an invocation cast into the depth of the catacomb.

Two of the robed figures stepped from the chanting semicircle and lifted Emily's limp body.

She remained unconscious, her head lolling back, her face ashen under the flickering torchlight as they secured her to the imposing boulder. The harsh scrape of the chains echoed in the chamber.

As she slumped against the cold stone, another roar came from the tunnel.

Closer now.

The Grendsluagh was coming. There was no time to concoct a perfect plan. They had to move. Now.

Time seemed to slow as Walker unzipped his pack, the sound disguised by the chanting.

He pulled out a jersey and indicated that Max and Laurel should do the same, although the two exchanged puzzled glances as they did so.

Then Max's eyes lit up with understanding.

She smiled as she quickly fished out a small fuel bottle from her pack, its metallic surface glinting in the torchlight.

Together, they built a small pile of clothing on the stone floor behind the pillar. Max unscrewed the top of the fuel bottle and shook its contents over the clothes. There wasn't much, but hopefully it would be enough to cause a distraction.

"You two go over to the other side, then I'll light it," she whispered. "Be ready for the distraction."

Another roar bellowed from the depths of the tunnel.

Walker and Laurel slipped away from the pillar and crept around the back of the chamber to hide on the opposite side, nearer the rock.

The echoes of chanting bounced off the walls of the chamber, spiralling toward a feverish crescendo.

Walker peered around the edge of the pillar to get a sense of how they might free Emily.

She stirred, raising her head a little, as her eyes flickered open. There was confusion in her gaze, then terror. Her eyes widened at the robed figures before her.

As she realised she was chained, Emily struggled, still weak from the drugs, straining at the bonds that held her to the rock.

Walker was desperate to run to her — but he held back, willing Max to hurry. This had to work.

Across the other side of the cavern, a thin, grey trail of smoke snaked out from behind a pillar.

Then it fanned into a thick plume of black, curling up toward the ceiling like a swirling fog.

"Help! Fire!" Max's shout pierced the chanting, her voice ringing out clear.

The robed figures wavered, their ritualistic harmony faltering.

Several of them spun toward the smoke, their cloaked forms illuminated by the eerie light. They seemed startled, confusion rippling through their ranks.

In their disarray, half of them abandoned their position and hurried to stop the flames. The other six remained resolute, their chants undeterred, focused on Emily and the tunnel behind her as the roar of the Grendsluagh rang out once more.

Suddenly, an aggressive clanging resonated through the chamber, echoing around so its source was unclear.

Walker spun to see Laurel at the very back of the cavern, pounding a climbing carabiner onto the metal of a flaming torch bracket.

Several more of the robed figures spun toward the sound, their attention successfully diverted.

Two of the robed figures remained, one holding a wooden staff.

Walker exploded from the shadows, rushing the two robed figures still fixated on Emily.

With a roar, he charged at the older figure, swinging his hefty hand torch with every ounce of his strength.

The torch connected with a sickening thud, sending the

figure sprawling to the ground in a heap of billowing robes.

As the figure rolled over and cowered on the ground, Walker glimpsed the older man's face with his bushy white eyebrows and walrus moustache.

The younger figure next to him, startled by the sudden onslaught, took a step back. His hood fell away, revealing a familiar face.

"Tom?" Walker gasped. Emily's boyfriend, the young man he'd met barely hours before. The bastard.

Walker lunged forward, his rage redoubled at the betrayal.

His knuckles connected with the younger man's midsection.

Tom doubled over and staggered back as Walker advanced.

"Dad!" Emily called out in desperation.

Walker whirled back toward his daughter.

As he reached for her, he was slammed from behind; the blow took him to his knees.

With a swift roll, Walker spun around, raising his arms in defence as the recovered older man attacked him with a wooden staff topped by the snarling head of a beast.

Walker launched himself at the older figure in a rugby tackle, and they both rolled on the floor. Walker shifted his weight to flip the man onto his back.

Just as he raised his fist to deliver a finishing blow, Tom, now recovered from Walker's initial assault, crashed into him. Their momentum sent them both sprawling away from the elder man.

As they wrestled on the floor, a terrifying roar rang out in the chamber, along with the sound of claws on rock.

The Grendsluagh was here.

CHAPTER 16

Time slowed to a crawl, the tumult of battle suspended as all turned toward the beast now entering the chamber.

Walker's eyes widened as he took in its horror.

It was a monstrous caricature of a man, its body massive and distorted. It was sheathed in a mottled, leathery hide that seemed to writhe under the flickering torchlight, as if the souls it had devoured still struggled to escape its form.

Its limbs ended in deadly talons that scratched against the stone floor, and its gaping jaws bristled with rows of sharp, needle-like teeth.

But for all its grotesque form, the Grendsluagh moved with a predatory grace. The shadows of the catacomb seemed to swirl around it as it advanced upon its prey, a foul stench filling the air as it stepped forward.

Emily screamed as she desperately tried to escape her chains.

The robed figures in the chamber dropped to their knees and began to chant once more in a desperate plea for deliverance, the words warped and twisted by the echoes in the vast chamber.

Walker felt Tom's grip relax. He rolled away quickly, springing up from the floor holding the wooden staff that the older man had dropped.

He shouted to attract the creature's attention. "Hey! Over here!"

He rushed at the Grendsluagh, swinging the staff in a wide arc, putting all his strength into the blow.

But the beast merely swiped at him with a taloned fist.

The powerful blow sent Walker sprawling back to the ground. The chamber tilted and whirled around him as he landed with a thud, winded, his breath hitching painfully in his chest.

The Grendsluagh turned once more to Emily, its leathery skin rippling as it flexed its talons.

Walker crawled forward, desperation driving him back toward his daughter.

"Hey!" Max shouted. She stepped out from behind a pillar, flaming torch held high. "Over here!"

The flames flickered and spat, casting monstrous shadows across her determined face as smoke billowed around her.

The Grendsluagh turned, its attention briefly shifting.

Walker staggered to his feet and scrambled to reach Emily — but once more the older man rushed him, using his bulk to pin Walker against the cold, unforgiving stone of the chamber wall.

The impact drove the breath once more from Walker's lungs.

"It must take her, for the good of us all." The old man's expression was grim, his grasp iron-hard with determination.

Over the man's shoulder, Walker watched the Grendsluagh twist around, the beast's focus drawn by their struggle.

Its glowing eyes narrowed. With a swift, fluid movement that belied its size, it took a step toward them, slicing its claw through the air, raking it diagonally across and down the back of the older man.

He screamed as the sound of tearing fabric and flesh echoed in the chamber.

Blood sprayed, staining the ancient stone as the man's body jolted violently in agony, his expression a mask of disbelief.

As his life drained away, his collapsing weight bore down on Walker, pinning him against the unyielding stone.

Walker strained to push the body away. His muscles screamed in protest as he heaved against the dead weight, the metallic tang of blood filling his nostrils.

Walker finally shoved the dead man off — just as several other robed figures set upon him. Unprepared for their sudden assault, he couldn't stop them from forcing him down onto the hard stone, pinning him down, their grip firm.

"Let me go, you bastards! Let me go!" He writhed and bucked, desperately trying to break free and reach his daughter.

The Grendsluagh roared once more.

It whirled around and reached for Emily, snapping her loose from the chains with one taloned hand.

She beat at it with her fists, screaming and writhing as it dragged her toward the dark tunnel beyond the boulder, moving surprisingly fast for its size.

"Daddy!" Her scream echoed in the chamber as the beast disappeared into the darkness, its sacrifice clutched in its talons.

"No! Emily!"

Walker thrashed beneath the weight of his captors, their fingers like iron bands around his flesh. His muscles strained to the breaking point, every fibre of his being screaming for him to fight, to break free, to reach Emily.

"There's no point in fighting now." The words were cold, delivered without emotion, a stark contrast to the surrounding chaos.

Tom knelt beside the lifeless body of his father, the older man's blood seeping into his robes, colouring them a deep crimson.

"It will take her down to its chamber in the depths and devour her." His voice was hollow as he cast a bitter glance toward the dark tunnel where the Grendsluagh had disappeared. "We have saved the city for another year, and that is worth her life."

Tom turned to look at Walker, and in his gaze was a dark promise. "But you will face justice for what you did here." He pointed to the body. "You murdered my father, leader of the Cabal and beloved chancellor of the university."

In an instant, Walker saw how his future might play out.

No one would believe his story, the Cabal would see to that. He would face chains, a courtroom, the loneliness of a jail cell, or an insanity ward — and his daughter would be lost to the creature in the depths.

He redoubled his efforts, wrestling the men that held him down, but they outnumbered him and Walker could not get free.

"Let him go." Laurel's voice echoed through the stone chamber. Her words hung in the air, a gauntlet thrown in the midst of chaos.

The robed figures paused, glancing at each other, uncertainty in their gaze as they parted to allow Laurel through.

She walked tall and proud, her eyes fixed on Tom and the body of the chancellor.

"We're going after Emily, and you're going to let us."

Tom's laugh reverberated around the chamber and his face twisted into a cruel smile as he gazed at Laurel.

"You're the librarian, right?" His tone was patronising, the voice of someone used to being in control. "You worked for my father. I'll implicate you too."

Laurel shook her head. "I know about the hidden chamber in the library, the paintings of the Grendsluagh, *The Codex of the Cabal and the Monstrous Accord*. I have photos, evidence of what you have all done."

She walked closer, her gaze fixed on his. "And I saw

you take Emily. I saw you together at the Spiegeltent, and I watched you push her into a van. I'm a witness to Emily's abduction and the abomination here tonight."

Tom reached out and grabbed her arm, the force of his grip making her gasp. His nails dug into her skin, threatening to break the surface.

But Laurel didn't flinch. "What are you going to do? Kill me too? Blame that on Walker as well?"

Her words echoed in the chamber, and her challenge hung in the air.

The robed figures shifted as they cast furtive glances at each other. Their whispers slithered around the chamber as uncertainty and collective unease spread at the threat of exposure.

They had managed to get away with one disappearance a year for centuries, but would this be too much to explain away?

With a gruff sound of irritation, Tom forcefully shoved Laurel away, dismissing her with a wave of his hand.

"Go after her then. The Grendsluagh will take you too, and we will be rid of you all."

The robed figures stepped away from Walker.

He pulled himself upright, even as his body ached from the blows of Grendsluagh and these men. Snatching up his discarded pack, he headed toward the ominous tunnel.

He nodded at Laurel and Max, who had now emerged to stand alongside them.

"Thank you, but you don't have to come with me. It's dangerous and I don't know what might happen."

Part of Walker wanted them to turn back, to be safe up in the city above. But the events of the night had bonded the three, and as the moment stretched, he willed the two women to join him.

"I'm with you." Laurel's voice was as steady as her gaze.

Max took a deep breath and then nodded. "Me too. Let's finish this."

She fell into step beside Walker and together, the three of them dashed into the tunnel after the Grendsluagh.

CHAPTER 17

FEAR AND ADRENALIN COURSED through Laurel's veins as she dashed into the tunnel after Walker, Max by her side, wondering what the hell she had just done. What had driven her to plunge into this seemingly hopeless situation?

Her mind whirled, flitting from the surreal confrontation with the robed figures to the potential fallout waiting for her back at the university if she ever made it out of here.

She would have to accuse the — now dead — chancellor and his son, a prominent student, of kidnapping as well as convince the authorities that a secret cult controlled the city. It would seem ludicrous to those on the surface, and by the time she made it back up there, Tom would have figured out his story. He would make sure she was destroyed. All in the defence of a man she'd barely even known a single night. Despair swept over her.

But then Laurel noticed the rock walls around her.

They were scarred with deep gouges from sharp talons, telltale signs of the monster's passage. It was a reminder of what awaited Emily when the Grendsluagh reached its lair.

Every year for who knew how many generations, the city had sent an innocent down here as a sacrifice. And for what? The prosperity and wealth of a few protected by the ignorance of the many. Edinburgh was not some utopia where all lived in abundance. The Cabal protected their own interests, and it was time to end the curse of generations.

Laurel jogged on after Walker with renewed determination. The rocky floor of the tunnel sloped downwards, and the air grew increasingly hot and stifling.

They must be getting closer to the heart of the volcano. She remembered from the map in the book that there were several levels between the Chamber of Offering and the Grendsluagh's dark sanctuary.

Walker halted suddenly and bent low, his torchlight casting an eerie glow over the rough stone floor.

Laurel skidded to a stop beside him, her breath coming in ragged gasps as she saw what had captured Walker's attention.

Droplets of blood splattered across the stone.

He surged ahead again, racing down the tunnel with renewed determination.

Laurel pushed off the tunnel wall and sprinted after him. She wasn't used to this much running and was struggling to keep up, her heart pounding too fast in her chest. She was a scholar, at home in the quiet and still comfort of her library, not cut out for this unyielding sprint into the unknown to face a monster of nightmare come to life.

Max was in front of her now, her lithe frame clearly at ease with the rhythm of movement, but she kept looking back to check Laurel was still there. The urbexer seemed to have pulled herself together after facing the trauma of the cave-in and then the creature in the lake. She could have walked away in the Chamber of Offering, but it seemed they were a team now, and they would leave no one behind.

After what seemed like an eternity, Walker and Max came to a halt at the end of the tunnel.

Laurel mustered the last of her energy to reach them, her thighs burning, her lungs aching for air. Leaning against the stone wall, she drew ragged breaths as she calmed her thumping heart.

Ahead of them, the tunnel opened up into a cavernous expanse. The edges disappeared into inky blackness, stretching far beyond the reach of their meagre lights.

But instead of the bare stone caverns they had navigated so far, this was like another world entirely.

The air was thick and humid, wrapping around Laurel and clinging to her lungs as she breathed. This was no normal cave climate, but an underground hothouse fuelled by the volcano's heat, teeming with strange, voracious life.

The sharp tang of warm earth and decaying vegetation filled the air, reminiscent of the loamy richness of a rainforest. There was an ominous rustling of leaves, the skitter of unseen insects, and the distant gurgling of water as a hidden underground river coursed through the heart of the subterranean ecosystem.

As her eyes adjusted to the gloom, Laurel took in the grotesque beauty of the cavern.

It was a twisted mirror of a lush, tropical jungle, rife with menacing, carnivorous plants whose vibrantly coloured tendrils swayed as if they sensed the presence of unfamiliar prey. Strange vines crept up from crevices, entwining with each other like grotesque serpents. Each was adorned with fleshy bulbs and monstrous flowers that bore an uncanny resemblance to torn human flesh. Even the thorns appeared like curved talons, ready to tear into any living thing that dared trespass.

The walls were covered with lichen in pallid, cadaverous hues — sickly yellow and bruised purple — which gave the stone a semblance of diseased flesh.

Max played her torch over the vegetation ahead. "How do we get through this?" She turned back to Laurel. "Or did we run past a side tunnel? Maybe this isn't even the way. Is there something in the book?"

As Laurel rummaged in her pack for the ancient tome, Walker crouched down near the plants at the entrance to the cavern.

"This is definitely the way." He pointed to droplets of crimson on the tendrils of a plant and on the stone below. "The blood is fresh. We have to press on."

"Wait." Laurel quickly paged through the book. "We need to be careful in this cavern."

She found a specific page and turned it round so the others could see an intricately drawn diagram of plants devouring a corpse. "There's a warning about this place. The plants are alive — and hungry. We have to be careful down there."

Her words echoed in the cavernous expanse, and as if in response to her revelation, a heavy rustling stirred in the vegetation beyond.

The vines seemed to pulsate, bulbs swelling and contracting as if inhaling their scent in the air. One of the flesh-flowers bloomed open, revealing a maw lined with sharp, teeth-like thorns just as an insect flew too close to the monstrous flower.

It snapped shut, trapping the insect inside to be slowly dissolved by the juices within. A trickle of vile green liquid ran down the side of the vine, glistening in the torchlight.

"Stay alert, stay close," Walker muttered, his face etched with grim determination as he stepped into the thick vegetation.

CHAPTER 18

Max trailed behind Walker and Laurel as they forged ahead into the vegetation. It was hot and densely humid, and as she stopped to take off her fleece and stuff it into her pack, she couldn't help but wonder at her surroundings.

The vibrant palette of riotous colour and variety of scents were overwhelming after the stark stone of the earlier tunnels. She had explored countless underground places, navigated abandoned mines and underground ruins. But this was a different kind of wasteland, its untamed flora a far cry from the quiet decay of human-made structures she was used to. This place had a grotesque beauty, and it was a unique spectacle that only a few daring — or desperate — explorers would ever witness.

Each plant was a kind of natural graffiti, daubing the cavern with nature's rebellious tag. Their shapes were as varied and peculiar as any urban art she had seen. There were twisted tendrils, leaves serrated like rusty barbed wire, and petals veined in an array of jarring hues.

Max itched to pull out her camera, longing to capture the eerie beauty of this carnivorous garden for her audience online. She imagined the original photographs she could take, with twisted shadows and the juxtaposition of raw, alien life against rugged stone.

Photography had always been her way of capturing the unseen beauty of the city's bones. Urbex wasn't just about the thrill of the breach, the adrenalin of trespass, but also about documenting what was left behind, the hidden aspects of the world most people never got to witness. Each photograph she posted online was also proof of her own journey, a piece of the urban tapestry she had woven over the years. This place would be a revelation for those who considered the depths beneath the city to be cold and forbidding — and she was desperate to show it to them.

As their makeshift path through the undergrowth weaved closer to one of the cavern walls, Max played her torch over the lichen that carpeted every inch in a miniature landscape of crags and valleys.

They were not of uniform growth but more a complex ecology of various species. Some bore tiny flowers of tainted hues, and others formed patterns that looked like faces contorted with terror. The vines that climbed the walls were dark twins of rainforest liana, their bulbs bloating and deflating with a rhythm that was almost hypnotic.

As Max leaned closer, another of the bulbs opened its flesh-like flower. An insect landed on its petal and crawled toward the nectar within.

The insect was the size of a clenched fist with a chitinous exoskeleton, as hard and jagged as shards of broken glass. Its wings were broad and leathery, resembling the dried leaves of the macabre plants around, and it was a deep, oily black, absorbing light in a way that made the creature seem like a moving shadow.

Six elongated legs sprouted from its underbelly, each ending in a set of barbed hooks, perfectly designed to latch onto and shred soft flesh. The insect moved with an uncanny, lurching motion, each step leaving behind a small pool of viscous, luminous fluid, creating an eerie glow in the darkness.

It was unlike anything she had seen before, and Max bit her lip as she wrestled with indecision.

She glanced ahead.

Walker and Laurel moved swiftly through the vegetation, fixed on the potential path ahead. There was surely time to take a few quick photos before they were out of sight. No one had ever documented this place and its bizarre life forms, and Max couldn't resist the urge to capture it.

She moved slowly, careful not to disturb the insect from its quest, and opened her pack. She pulled out her tiny digital camera.

Holding her breath, Max looked through the viewfinder and focused on the unusual insect, every detail sharp in the frame.

She took shot after shot, shifting her position so she could capture different angles. Her hip brushed against one plant as she tried to include more of the cave as a backdrop.

Suddenly, a sharp, searing pain on her forearm cut through her concentration.

Max let out a surprised gasp.

She dropped her camera as she flinched away from the hideous vine that was now wrapped around her arm, its barbed tendrils embedded into her skin. The thorns gleamed, slick with her blood, and they flexed as if alive to secure their grip upon her. A burning sensation spread from the wounds, as if the vine were pumping venom into her veins.

"Help!" Her shout reverberated around the cavern. "Walker! Laurel!"

Max desperately tried to wrench the plant off, but the vine tightened its grip, the venomous thorns digging deeper as she moaned with pain. Other vines curled closer to her feet as if to pull her to the ground and smother her.

Laurel and Walker whirled around. They crashed back through the undergrowth to reach her, squelching the fleshy plants underfoot, releasing a pungent rotten odour that turned the stomach.

Walker pulled out his knife and hacked at the sinewy stem of the monstrous flower below Max's arm, as Laurel tried to fend off the other advancing vines. Max whimpered as the thorns burrowed deeper, injecting more of the numbing poison into her veins.

With a grunt of effort and a last brutal hack, Walker severed the bulbous vine.

It softened and fell away, leaving a bloodied, gaping wound on Max's arm.

She collapsed to the cavern floor, her breath coming in short, pained gasps.

Laurel knelt next to her. "Do you have a first aid kit?"

"In… my… bag," Max gasped, her vision narrowing as the venom infused her veins.

Laurel hastily pulled out the first aid kit and Max nodded at the antihistamine tablets.

"Give me one of those first. It might slow any allergic reaction."

Laurel quickly gave her the tablet, along with a couple of strong painkillers, and Max dry swallowed them as Laurel took out an antiseptic wipe. She removed as much of the plant material as she could, then sprayed the open wound with antiseptic before wrapping it in a bandage.

Max gritted her teeth at the pain, but the open wound didn't worry her as much as whatever the hell was in the plant's toxin.

"We need to move." Walker slashed at the vines that writhed toward the three of them. "The scent of fresh blood in the air has set this place off."

The verdant garden around them quivered as the plants transformed into a writhing carpet of predatory hunger. Vines snaked toward them with alarming speed, thorn-encrusted tendrils twitching in anticipation.

Above them, the lichen-covered ceiling trembled, releasing a cloud of insects.

They descended like a plague, darkening the air as some spun down on silken threads while others scuttled down the walls with a chitinous rattle.

CHAPTER 19

"Let's go!" Walker bent to help Max up, dragging her through the undergrowth as Laurel took her other arm, both propelling her on.

The ground was alive beneath their feet, bucking and churning as roots erupted from the ground to twist up around their ankles as they passed. The plants writhed and lunged, coiled and twisted, fighting to ensnare their prey once more.

Bulbous flowers snapped at their heels. Gaping maws revealed rows of serrated teeth as viscous venom dripped from the hungry petals, the substance sizzling where it splattered their clothes.

Walker slashed with his blade, leaving Max to lean on Laurel as he defended their escape route, severing the advancing tendrils that sought to ensnare them.

The teeming cloud of insects soon reached them. They dive-bombed the three, peppering their exposed skin with stinging bites, their frenzy fuelled by the tantalising scent of fresh blood.

Max could barely breathe as they staggered through the undergrowth, her heart thundering from the exertion of trying to run and the assault of the venom. As her vision narrowed, she noticed that the sound of running water was growing louder.

They burst out of the jungle onto the edge of a series of steep stone steps that led down to a subterranean river. The water was fast and furious, a torrent of churning white froth that rushed toward what sounded like a waterfall in the distance.

The steps were slick with a carpet of damp moss, which lent an uncanny luminescence to the surfaces in the spectral glow of bioluminescent fungi clinging to the cavern ceiling. Rivulets of water traced paths along the edge of the steps, cascading down in miniature waterfalls.

As Max looked down the steep stairs that lead to the roaring river below, a knot of foreboding tightened in her stomach.

Her head spun, and the world tilted precariously as venom pulsed through her veins, clouding her vision with splinters of pain. As the strength in her limbs waned, a heavy lethargy pulled her down, as if trying to root her to the spot. She only wanted to sink down right here and rest, but they had to press on.

Max leaned on Laurel, depending on her strength to stay upright, but even that might not be enough. She could only hope the drugs would kick in soon and she could walk on under her own power. She couldn't ask Walker to wait as time was running out for Emily.

Behind them, he fought against the relentless onslaught of the carnivorous vines, grunting with effort.

Each slice of his knife through the sinewy stems sent a spray of plant ichor splattering onto the mossy stone beneath them. His breathing was a harsh reminder that they would not last long here. They had to get to the water, where the garden's domain ended.

"We can make it," Laurel said with determination. "One step at a time."

"I'll stay behind you and keep the plants off," Walker called back.

With a last look back at the encroaching vines, Max drew a shaky breath and steeled herself for the descent.

Each stride was a battle. Her legs threatened to buckle beneath her on the unyielding stone. The steps were slippery beneath her feet, damp with rivulets of water and treacherously slick moss. The throb of pain in her arm was a relentless drumbeat, pulsing in sync with her racing heart, and the world around her spun and swayed.

Laurel supported her as much as possible with her arm a steady brace around Max's waist. Every time Max stumbled, Laurel tightened her grip, steadying her with a determined tenacity while Walker protected their descent from behind.

At last, the steps ended in a flat expanse of stone that jutted out into the furious torrent of water. Max's strength gave out, and she slumped down, resting her burning arm in the shallow froth that lapped over the edge of the platform.

Laurel knelt beside her, their breath mingling in ragged gasps.

Walker joined them a moment later, sweat dripping down his face, his clothes covered in green slime and snagged with thorny pieces of vine.

But the violent attack was over.

"I have to push on," Walker said once he had caught his breath. He pointed over the rushing river. "It's not too wide and presumably not too deep, since the Grendsluagh must have come this way with Emily. There's no other way through that cavern."

He rose to his feet, his gaze intent on the turbulent water that separated them from their path ahead, then looked back at Max. "Can you make it?"

She glanced up at the writhing vines on the upper steps. "Well, I'm not going back that way."

Laurel gave a short laugh. "Me neither. Onwards it is."

Walker strode into the water. The river swirled up around his waist as he braced himself against the current and tested the bottom depth until he found purchase below.

Turning back to the shore, he extended a hand toward Max. "It's not too deep. Come on. We can make it together."

He helped her down. The freezing shock of the water was a blessed relief on Max's arm as the icy coolness soothed the inflamed wound.

Laurel clambered in behind her and together they began to walk across, fighting the insistent tug of the current sideways toward the waterfall.

Max kept her uninjured hand on Walker's pack to anchor herself, but each step was a struggle, each breath a battle.

She pressed on, sensing Laurel pushing her from behind, grateful for support on either side. The three of them had been strangers earlier today, and now it seemed they would risk their lives for each other.

By the time they made it to the middle of the river, they moved in unison. Inch by painstaking inch, they shuffled forward, keeping their feet anchored to the ground. Their clothes clung, heavy with water, to almost numb limbs, but they pushed on.

The roar of the waterfall grew louder as they made it into the final metres, the shore growing closer with each strained step.

As Max gave in to relief at the sight of the nearby shore, a sudden rush of debris tumbled across the surface of the water. Twigs and foliage, then small branches torn from unseen trees upstream, bobbed and tumbled toward them in the frothing current.

She braced herself against the onslaught of the debris, letting go of Walker's pack so it could pass between them.

Behind her, Laurel let go too.

Suddenly, a huge log loomed out of the darkness like a missile; thick branches angled out from either side as it plunged down the river toward them.

Walker spun around, instinctively reaching out to grab Max's arm.

She clung to him and turned to grab for Laurel — their fingers brushed for a fleeting moment—

The log crashed into them.

They were torn apart.

The current yanked Laurel away as if she were nothing more than another piece of driftwood. Her scream was cut off as she disappeared beneath the surface, swallowed by the torrential current — hurtling toward the waterfall.

CHAPTER 20

Laurel's world turned to chaos. One moment, she was fighting against the biting cold of the rushing water, her boots scrabbling for purchase on the slick, submerged stones.

The next, the log hit her, knocking her sideways.

The turbulent current tugged her off her feet, water flooding her mouth with the bitter taste of minerals and chalk as she gasped in shock.

She fought against the barrelling flow, flailing her arms, kicking her legs to prevent herself from being tangled in the branches of the log that still tumbled around her.

But the torrent flowed on, carrying her downstream as it tossed her body about like a rag doll.

The sound of the waterfall grew louder. Her panic rose.

Laurel kicked out for the bank, swimming as hard as she could at a diagonal to the current, each stroke a battle, each breath a victory.

The desperate struggle against the torrential water was exhausting, but Laurel mustered every ounce of strength she had. She kicked against the rapids, reaching out for the slippery stones of the bank, the roots of plants, anything that would offer an anchor.

But the savage current was relentless.

She fought to keep her head above the surface, gasping for air between the frothing waves.

Her body hit something hard and unyielding. A submerged boulder. The force of the collision sent pain lancing through her, a burning ache spreading like wildfire across her ribs. Laurel could taste coppery blood in her mouth, the sharp tang of it mixing with the acrid taste of the river.

She glimpsed a low-hanging branch jutting out from the bank.

With a final, desperate surge of energy, she lunged toward it, fingers brushing the coarse bark—

But the merciless water ripped her away before she could secure a hold.

The branch slipped from her reach, her final chance of salvation snatched away.

Her struggle became a blur as the roar of the waterfall grew deafeningly loud. The world tilted, her vision filled with the churn and froth of the waterfall's edge.

It might as well be the edge of her world.

Laurel took a deep breath as she plunged over the waterfall, her scream swallowed by the thunderous sound of the cascading water.

* * *

Max watched in horror as Laurel disappeared into the dark, carried away by the merciless torrent.

Walker pulled her on toward the bank, but Max resisted. "We have to go in after her."

"We can't. We'll only get pulled in, too." He pointed at the boulders alongside. "But she might have found a way onto the bank. If we stay out of the water, we might be able to get to her."

Max's arm throbbed painfully in response to the tussle,

the once intense burn now spreading into a cold numbness that was beginning to creep up her shoulder.

Her strength was waning — but they had to go after Laurel. She might be clinging to the bank just out of sight. The librarian had helped both Max and Walker, and they owed her this.

"Can you manage?" Walker's concerned gaze took in the pallor of her face and the tremor in her clenched fist.

Max nodded. "You go in front. I'll follow behind."

Walker edged precariously along the rugged bank of the river, clambering over treacherous rocks slick with river algae along the water's edge. Max stayed as close behind as she could, using her good arm to brace against boulders while holding the injured one close to her chest.

A silver flash rippled through the water just metres away.

Max flinched back with a sharp intake of breath — but it was just the underside of another branch, not the tentacle of the nightmare from the lake.

She hurried after Walker, who was now a little way ahead. In her haste, she slipped on the wet stones and jolted her injured arm. A sharp, biting pain made her clench her teeth, but she would not cry out.

There was no sign of Laurel, so they kept on along the edge of the bank, desperately hoping for some sign of her.

The sound of the waterfall reverberated through the cavern. It grew louder with every step and soon they found themselves on the edge of a precipice.

The thundering river was now a shimmering curtain of water that tumbled into the abyss. The booming roar of the waterfall vibrated through Max's bones as the spray from the falls created a fine mist that clung to their clothes.

They stood close to the brink and looked down into the frothing white water that seemed to dissolve into spectral mist as it plummeted into the inky darkness below.

CHAPTER 21

For Laurel, the fall seemed to last an eternity, the world around her a blur of rushing water and icy terror — until she plunged into the deep pool below the drop.

The impact drove the air from her lungs, and she tumbled in the wash as the pressure of the waterfall kept her submerged.

Her lungs screamed for air, her vision tunnelling.

She fought against the downward pressure, struggling to kick her way back to the surface.

Summoning the last remnants of her strength, Laurel swam down and away from the churning fury. Her muscles ached and her lungs burned. Just as she was about to give up, she broke the surface, sucking in ragged breaths as her body shook with the effort.

The roar of the waterfall echoed around her, drowning out the harsh sound of her gasps. She swam toward the edge of the pool, her hands scrabbling for purchase on the slick rocks.

She dragged herself onto the rocky shore, coughing and spluttering, her body trembling with exhaustion from her efforts. Thankfully, it was warmer down here and the rocks emitted a welcome heat. This chamber must be closer to the heart of the volcano.

Laurel lay for a moment as she recovered, letting her heartbeat slow and her lungs fill with oxygen once more.

Above her, clusters of glow-worms spun over the ceiling. Like a scattered constellation of tiny stars, their soft, ethereal light cast an otherworldly glow in the cavern.

Her body ached, but it could have been a lot worse. Laurel pushed the dark thoughts away and wondered if Max and Walker had followed or whether they had carried on, assuming she was lost.

Either way, she had to find a way out of here.

Her pack floated in the pool nearby and she fished it out. She'd lost her head torch in the churning water, but she still had a hand torch inside. The ancient book was damp, but her pack had mostly protected it.

Laurel shone the torch around her, illuminating the edges of the cave, daring to hope there might be a way out that did not involve climbing back up that waterfall.

On first glance, it looked like there was nothing — but then she saw a discolouration on the rock face to one side.

Laurel pushed up to her hands and knees, reeling a little as dizziness threatened to become nausea. She took a few more deep breaths and then crawled across the rocks, taking her time to place her hands carefully so she didn't fall again.

When she reached the rock face, Laurel discovered a fissure. The discolouration was a crack in the rock big enough to slip through.

She shone her torch into the crevice.

The dim, spectral light reflected off piles of bones that littered the ground.

Human bones.

* * *

Walker inched his way closer to the edge of the waterfall, the rocks beneath his feet growing slicker and more treacherous with each step.

He peered over the edge and scanned the pool of frothing white below.

But there was only water. No corpse floated on its surface.

Either Laurel lay pinned at the bottom of the pool by the weight of the falls, or she was trapped under branches, hidden in the darkness behind them. Either way, she was gone.

A wave of guilt swept over Walker. He shouldn't have let her come with him. He shouldn't have let either of them. Max was badly injured, Laurel might be drowned, and every second that passed made Emily's death more likely.

For a moment, Walker felt like letting go. He could just topple forward and it would be over. He was no stranger to the pull of shadow, but he had resisted it before by visualising Emily. Now, he had to hold on to the thought of seeing her again — while there was still a chance to save her.

A flash of sudden torchlight in the cavern below drew his gaze.

"There, look!" Max grabbed his arm and pointed. "She's alive."

Relief flooded over Walker, and he couldn't help but give a wry smile. The librarian was certainly surprising.

"Laurel! Laurel!" they shouted together, but the tumult of the water drowned their voices and there was no way she could see them up here.

They watched as the torchlight slowly made its way along the shore and then disappeared.

Walker turned to Max. "We have to get down there."

Her pinched expression and the way she held her arm showed she was in a lot of pain, but she was also used to exploring alone underground. The urbexer was resilient. She didn't need rescuing. Given his level of exhaustion after the challenges so far, Walker wondered at his own ability to climb down — but they had to reach Laurel and then go after Emily. They needed to get deeper into the heart of the catacomb, so perhaps they might even reach it more quickly this way.

Walker knelt down and examined the route. It would not be swift or easy. Jagged rocks slick from the spray of the waterfall could serve as footholds and support but could just as easily result in injury — or worse — if either of them fell.

They had no choice.

"I'll go first," Walker said. "Use me for extra support as we climb down and if you fall, well, maybe I can stop us both from ending up in the pool below."

Max grimaced as she gazed down at the escarpment. "It might be quicker to jump, you know."

Walker turned to face the rock and eased himself over the edge, feeling for a foothold, and then slowly lowering himself down.

The uneven surface of the rock was a jigsaw of crevices and outcrops, a puzzle that demanded concentration as he shifted his weight, keeping three points of contact on the rock at all times.

His muscles burned, his whole body aching from the fight in the cave and the challenges they had faced so far. He breathed through it and, with each exhale, he inched further down, following the path of the water, his body pressed tight against the wall.

Above him, Max followed suit.

She grappled with the rock face, taking most of the strain on her legs and good arm, demonstrating her climbing capability. But despite her years of urbexing, Walker could see her limbs shaking with a combination of effort and the cold spray that poured over the falls. It painted rivulets down the rock face, its path winding and unpredictable, just like their treacherous descent.

A sudden yelp from above.

Max's boot slipped off a treacherous patch of moss-covered stone.

Walker launched himself up and wedged his shoulder underneath her foot, his heart hammering as she teetered on the brink.

Her weight jolted through him. As his muscles strained, he hugged the rock face even tighter, bracing himself as she scrabbled for a new foothold. She clawed for purchase against the wet rock, her breath coming in ragged gasps.

Finally, her boot found a stable crevice, and she pushed herself up against the stone face, supporting her own weight once more.

Once he was sure of her stability, Walker continued the descent, both of them moving even more slowly now.

In the last few metres of the descent, the roar of the waterfall grew louder still. A fine mist obscured the cavern floor as steam rose from cold water meeting hot stone.

It was difficult to see where the rock face ended, but finally, Walker's boot met solid ground once more.

He stepped down onto the flat and reached up to help Max.

She met his gaze. "Thank you."

Walker could tell she wasn't used to working in a team, but he had felt every bit as grateful for her help back in the first cave-in. Their unlikely team had an unspoken pact — they would not abandon each other now.

As they crossed the cave, Max's boot grazed a loose stone. It skittered across the cavern floor, clattering against the rock wall in front of a fissure.

A moment later, Laurel looked out of the crevice, her expression anxious — and then delighted.

She rushed out and threw her arms around them both, pulling them all into a team hug. "I thought I'd lost you, but thank goodness you're here."

She pulled away and pointed into the fissure. "You have to see this."

CHAPTER 22

Laurel shone her torch back into the crevice and led Walker and Max inside.

The naturally formed cave had been turned into an ossuary of sorts, with several piles of human bones. But they weren't haphazardly strewn as one would expect in a site of carnage. The Grendsluagh clearly did not devour its victims here. Instead, the bones were ritualistically arranged into geometric patterns and curious forms in a dark artistry that surely stretched back generations.

Drawings of the Grendsluagh covered the cave walls. Some were faded, others in fresher colours, all with sharp talons and an immense body of muscle and shadow. Most looked as if they had been scrawled with desperate haste, the intensity of the work suggesting a frantic need to warn those who entered here.

As Max sank to the floor to gather her strength, Walker joined Laurel in exploration. They shone their torches around, shadows weaving together over the cave walls, warping the carvings into monstrous inhuman figures that seemed to snarl from the rock face. Every depiction of the creature was a little different, yet each triggered a primal terror.

"This is not the monster's lair," Laurel said. "It's more like a sepulchre, maintained for the honoured dead, those offered in sacrifice."

She leaned closer to one etching. Her torchlight playing over the stone's rough surface illuminated a snapshot of violence, frozen in time and solidified in stone. The brutality of it made her shudder.

"It must be safe enough from the creature here for whoever makes these images and sculptures, but also close enough to retrieve the bones. Its lair can't be far."

As Laurel shone her torchlight around the cave, one particular section caught her eye. The scene was oddly out of place, a reversal of the others. The Grendsluagh cowered before a hooded priest holding a dark talisman high above its head.

Laurel frowned. The talisman bore a striking resemblance to something...

She swiftly rummaged in her pack, then triumphantly withdrew the artefact. She had completely forgotten about it since the library when she had picked it up along with the book.

Laurel handed the stone to Walker, noticing again how the polished, dark surface seemed to absorb the light. "I think it's obsidian — volcanic glass that forms when lava cools rapidly."

Walker ran his finger over the hole at the top of the piece. "Perhaps it comes from the heart of this ancient volcano, the place where the Grendsluagh emerged? Or at least where it lives now."

"By the looks of the drawing, the obsidian can control it or at least drive it back. Perhaps we can use it to rescue Emily."

"We just need to find her." Walker shone his torch over the walls and up to the ceiling. "But how the hell do we get out of here?"

* * *

Max leaned back against the warm stone of the cave wall.

She appreciated the volcanic heat as her body shook with the aftermath of the climb — and the venom. Her injured arm throbbed with the rhythm of her pulse in a hot, searing pain that threatened to overwhelm her with its intensity.

She pulled open her pack and dug into the first aid kit again, taking a couple more painkillers. They might dull the sensation for a little longer, but there was no way she was climbing back up that waterfall. If the only way out was the way they came in, then her bones would end up alongside these piles.

As Walker wondered aloud how they might get out, Max turned her attention to the problem.

Urban exploration had taught her many things — most importantly, to perceive her environment not as static, but as a layered narrative written in rust, stone, and time. Perhaps the same might apply to the more organic and primeval surroundings of this cave.

Her eyes adjusted to the dim torchlight, taking in the minutiae of the cavern that would otherwise go unnoticed.

Patches of fungal growth clung to the damp stone walls. Their organic patterns cut a stark contrast against the hard, unforgiving mineral surface. The tiny ecosystems were a testament to the cave's consistent humidity and the abundant nutrients from the ancient volcano eruption hidden within its craggy walls.

Max noticed stalactites and stalagmites in the corners of the cavern, their shapes moulded by the slow drip of water over centuries, depositing layer upon layer of minerals. Some of the taller formations bore the scars of erosion, their surfaces roughened and pitted. If water had made its way down here for so long, there was a path out. All they had to do was find it.

The rock layers of the cave walls revealed more of the story, with hints of rust and ochre streaking the stone, indicating traces of iron and other minerals.

The strata were angled in one direction. As she followed their path, Max noticed a thin, meandering fracture slicing through the stone and widening the higher up it went. Volcanic activity had cracked the rocks repeatedly over eons. This could be a fault line leading to nowhere, or it could lead on to the volcanic depths — and the Grendsluagh's lair.

Grimacing with the pain of her injured arm, Max pushed herself up from the floor. She crossed to the base of the fracture, and with gentle fingers, she skimmed the rough stone, tracing the ragged edges of the fracture.

A gust of warmer air brushed against her hand, hinting at a hidden cavity behind the solid facade of rock. Her years of experience told her there was something here worth investigating.

Walker's voice broke her focus. "What is it?" he asked, curiosity etching lines across his weathered face as he joined her below the crevice.

He reached out, his hand hovering just above hers. His eyes widened as he too felt the inexplicable surge of warmth.

His torchlight danced across the ragged stone as he aimed the beam upwards along the fracture, throwing it into stark relief.

"Do you think there's a way through up there? Perhaps the fissure widens at the top?"

"I need to get higher up to take a look," Max concluded, her gaze fixed on the tantalising hint of a passageway above veiled in shadow.

Walker crouched down, intertwining his strong fingers to create a makeshift step. "I'll give you a boost."

She clambered onto his offered hands and he lifted her, his arms straining with the effort. As she rose, Max reached up with her good arm, but her fingertips only scraped the edge of the fissure. It was close, but not close enough.

"Can you hoist me up just a bit more?" she called out to Walker, feeling the tension in his body as he pushed her higher.

Her fingers found tiny protrusions in the rock, a minute ledge barely enough to hook her fingertips around. It was small and rough, and if she had not been injured, it might have been enough.

But not today.

She had already pushed her body to its limits. She had little left to give.

"I can't reach it," Max admitted, biting her lip in frustration. "Not with my arm like this."

CHAPTER 23

"We just need to get you up another metre or so," Laurel said. "I can see how close you are…"

She scanned the room, then pointed at several large, misshapen boulders lying clustered in one corner. "We might be able to use these?"

Walker bent to allow Max to clamber off, and they gathered around the hulking rocks. While it might work, the thought of rolling them over to the fissure seemed almost impossible to Max.

But then the thought of staying here was just as unimaginable.

She sighed. "Perhaps if we push together?"

The boulders were as heavy as they looked, and the rough, gnarled surfaces didn't make the task any easier.

The three of them grunted and heaved and swore with the effort, but gradually the boulders started to shift.

Slowly but surely, they built a makeshift platform of stone beneath the fissure. It was a precarious balance of boulders, but it was enough to elevate Walker to a considerable height.

He clambered on top of the rock pile and extended a hand to help Max ascend.

Once again, he hoisted her onto his shoulders and she stretched up, determined to reach the crevice this time.

The additional height of the boulders brought her right up to the crevice, but she couldn't see very far into it, even with the torchlight.

"I need to go inside a little way. Can you boost me just a little further, Walker?"

As his strength propelled her up and in, Max gritted her teeth against the searing lance of pain that erupted from her injured arm. Ignoring the discomfort, she stretched out, her fingers finding purchase on the uneven rock inside the crevice.

With a final push, she hoisted herself into the narrow tunnel.

A rush of warmer air met Max as she slid further inside. The close quarters intensified the heat that emanated from the surrounding rock as she crept into the belly of the ancient volcano.

But it wasn't just the temperature that intensified as she crawled along. The air stank of rotting flesh and the metallic tang of blood. With every inch, Max felt more afraid of what she might find ahead.

She wriggled on through the tunnel.

It was a mosaic of fractured rock, each break and fissure a testament to the power of tectonic shifts over time. There were signs of once molten lava having cooled and solidified, its crystalline structure glittering like a night sky strewn with stars. Under her torchlight, it was reminiscent of the obsidian talisman that Laurel now carried.

Another time, Max might have lingered to examine it further, but now she forced herself on, pushing with her toes and pulling with her fingertips.

Minutes later, her head torch illuminated a gaping hole a little further on.

She clambered to its edge and froze as her light illuminated the cavern beyond. Her breath hitched in her throat, and she let out a soft gasp, her fingers clenching around the edge of the crevice.

The cavern yawned wide and deep, a cathedral of the underworld with a vaulted ceiling lost in the impenetrable darkness overhead. Bones lay strewn across the floor in a macabre mosaic, gnawed and broken into sharp pieces, scattered in discarded piles along with tattered remnants of clothing.

The Grendsluagh's lair.

This had been their goal all along, but now they were so close, Max could barely breathe. Maybe she could just inch back into the cave and tell Laurel and Walker that the way was blocked? She would even climb that damn waterfall if she had to, just to avoid stepping down into this basilica of bones.

She took a deep breath as she forced down her fear and doubt. They had to press on, but first Max needed a way to help Laurel and Walker out of the ossuary cave and into this tunnel.

She shone her torch light upwards, looking for a potential anchor point for a rope pulley.

The ceiling was alive with the fluttering, darting forms of bats roused from their slumber by her light. There were hundreds, possibly thousands, of them roosting above.

Several of them took flight, their shrill squeals echoing in the cavern as their wings beat the air, swirling near Max's face. She brushed them away with a shiver of revulsion.

They would need to stay quiet or the colony might swarm.

The tunnel was too tight to turn around in, so Max shuffled backwards a little way so she could call out to Laurel and Walker without disturbing the bats too much.

"This is definitely the way, but you're going to need help getting up here. I need to rig a rope. Walker, toss my bag up, then boost Laurel to the entrance and I'll feed the rope back so you can climb out of there."

The plan was good enough, and it was a relief to focus on something practical instead of the pain in her arm and her fear of what lay ahead.

"Okay," Walker called back. "I'm tossing the pack up now."

Max felt her bag land near her foot with a clink of metal on stone.

She hooked her ankle around it and crawled forward to the lair once more, this time dropping down onto the cavern floor.

She landed with a crunch of bone and grimaced as she tried not to imagine what lay beneath her boot. She scanned the cavern for a suitable anchor point. A heavy boulder with rocky outcrops covered in bat guano looked good enough.

Max looped the rope around one of the sturdy protrusions, tied a secure knot, and then leaned back with all her weight to test the setup.

The rope strained, pulling taut against the knot, but the boulder didn't shift. It would hold. It would be sturdy enough for Walker to climb out of the cave with.

There was a scrabbling noise and then a shower of stones at the tunnel exit. Laurel poked her head out in the chamber and her face blanched white as she saw what lay within.

Max put a finger to her lips and pointed up at the bats. "Stay quiet," she whispered. She heaved the end of the rope up to Laurel. "Pass this back to Walker."

Laurel nodded and disappeared once more. Within a few minutes, she returned, this time with Walker close behind.

They dropped down into the cavern and looked around. In the torchlight, Max saw the desolation on Walker's face as he realised his daughter's bones might be here amongst the dead.

A sudden, ferocious roar echoed through the cavern.

It came from the side opposite of where they stood. They spun around in the direction of the thunderous sound, torch beams slicing through the darkness.

The Grendsluagh was in the next cavern.

CHAPTER 24

As the monstrous roar echoed through the chamber, the colony of bats took flight.

They dive-bombed the three intruders, swarming them in a chaotic vortex of leathery wings and high-pitched squeals.

Walker and Laurel ran toward the Grendsluagh's roar, hands over their heads to try to protect themselves.

Max bent closer to the floor, ducking and running to the side of the cavern for shelter, her heart hammering in her chest. The bats teemed around her.

One landed and tried to scrabble inside her clothes.

She tore it off, the furry body and sharp claws making her almost hyperventilate. The creatures clearly had a taste for human flesh, and her wounded arm must be giving off a scent they craved.

More of them flew around her in a whirling mass, the stink of their musk mingling with the rotting flesh and dusty guano below, intensifying as they converged.

Walker and Laurel called for her. "Max! Max!"

But their voices echoed off the cavern walls, distant and muffled by the wingbeats of the frenzied swarm so she couldn't tell which direction they were in.

Max swung her uninjured arm in wide arcs to try to fend off the swooping creatures. Every breath was a hard-won battle, her sharp intakes of air interspersed with rapid, ragged exhalation, her movements hindered by injury.

She tried to focus, straining to catch the intermittent flicker of torches amidst the swirling, shrieking chaos.

But Walker and Laurel's shouts were muffled and distorted, like distant echoes beneath the cacophony. It was hard to know which way to go — but she had to move.

Max staggered in what she thought was the right direction — but in her haste, her boot slipped on a patch of guano on the cave floor.

She fell, sprawling to the ground, skidding into a pile of bones.

The impact jarred her injured arm, forcing a gasp of pain from her lips as the sharp edges of gnawed fragments dug into her skin.

As Max pushed herself up out of the dusty remains, she saw something she recognised. Half a metre away, beyond a half-broken skull, a backpack lay amongst the scattered bones, along with faded and shredded clothes.

Max's heart thumped with recognition.

She reached out a trembling hand and turned the pack around.

The sewn-on patch was grimy with dust and dark smudges of what might have been blood, but the image was still clear. A raised fist with middle finger extended.

It was Naomi's backpack — and Max lay sprawled in her remains.

She jerked back in horror, tears welling. She had known that Naomi was gone, but now she knew for sure that her friend met her fate at the monster's hands.

The bats still swarmed her, but Max no longer cared. She closed her eyes as guilt and grief for the loss of her friend swept over her.

"Max! Where are you? We have to go on." Walker's tone was urgent, clearly desperate to go after his daughter.

But Max couldn't move.

Her limbs were heavy, and her wounded arm throbbed, pulsating in a painful rhythm that beat in time with her racing heart. She suddenly realised that the sensation had spread, and now it was as if her entire arm was scoured with hot coals. Gritting her teeth and terrified of what she might see, Max shone the torch onto her arm.

The wound was an angry gash, the edges raw and inflamed with a mix of pus and blood seeping from it. Black lines weaved their way up her arm under the skin like the tendrils of some malevolent creature, as if the darkness of the cavern itself had invaded her flesh.

If she didn't get medical help soon, she might as well lie down here and become one with the remains of the dead.

Max knew she would only be a hindrance to Walker and Laurel, and she didn't want them distracted by protecting her as well as trying to rescue Emily. They would be better off without her.

"Go on ahead," she called out. "I'm right behind you."

* * *

Even as Max's words reached them, the roar of the Grendsluagh came again.

Walker picked up a broken femur as a makeshift weapon, its end sharp and pointed like a sword. He spun and raced into the tunnel leading out of the cavern, Laurel right behind.

The steep angle of the descent helped them run ever faster.

The air was thick with oppressive heat and the stench of sulphur and rotting meat. The stink of animal musk almost made Walker gag as they sprinted on, sweat pouring down their bodies.

The tunnel finally opened out into a massive chamber.

The ceiling, a twisted mass of blackened rock, loomed

high above. The floor beneath their feet was uneven and treacherous, jagged boulders jutting out like the teeth of some primordial beast. Along the walls, strange lichen clung to the stone, pulsating in hues of sickly green and putrid yellow.

At the chamber's centre, a churning, molten abyss spewed forth angry sparks and spurts of flame. A boiling pit of lava in the heart of the ancient volcano.

The surrounding air shimmered and wavered like a nightmare mirage as flickering light from the lava pit illuminated the monster that stood before it.

The Grendsluagh was a monstrous abomination born of darkness and chaos, a grotesque fusion of man and demon. It turned toward them, jagged talons poised to strike, its twisted face contorting as it roared in anger at their trespass.

At its feet, Emily lay prone. Her eyes were closed, her body battered and bruised, her clothes bloody.

CHAPTER 25

Time slowed.

As a bead of sweat trickled down Walker's face and stung his eyes, he was back in the burning tomb. The screams of his dying team echoed around him. The lick of flame scorched his skin.

Panic rose like an uncontrollable wave. His vision narrowed, and he collapsed against the wall, falling to his knees as the strength left his limbs.

Laurel crouched next to him and grabbed his shoulders, shaking him. "Walker! Snap out of it! Emily's alive. She's breathing. I can see her chest rise and fall."

The Grendsluagh roared once more.

It stepped over Emily's prone body, its eyes locked on the intruders. It advanced, taloned limbs ready to rip them apart.

But Walker couldn't move. He was transfixed by the flames and the creature mutated from the heart of the volcano as it strode toward them.

Laurel tore her pack off, opened the flap.

She pulled out the obsidian talisman and held it before her in the same way they had seen in the ossuary cavern.

"Get back!" she shouted, her voice lost in the roar of the flames.

The beast howled in frustration and took a step back.

It clenched its talons as it circled to one side, clearly trying to find a way to reach them.

As Laurel held the talisman aloft, she kicked Walker sharply in the leg. "Get up! I'll keep it away from you, but you have to get to Emily."

The pain of the blow permeated Walker's panic, and the fiery world coalesced once more into the cavern — with his daughter at its heart.

He dragged himself up the wall, coughing as he breathed in the foul air but regaining his strength with every moment.

Laurel darted forward, her movements agile and swift.

She thrust the obsidian talisman at the Grendsluagh. The monster recoiled from its strange power; a tortured snarl ripped from its malformed throat.

Walker took his chance.

He ran toward Emily's prone body as Laurel stayed near him, holding the talisman out to keep the creature at bay.

The Grendsluagh let out a guttural roar that shook the foundations of the chamber. It circled away, its speed surprising for its size. It clambered up the side of the rock face, limbs anchoring it to the blackened stone, and traversed swiftly around the back of the lava pit.

Laurel couldn't get to Walker fast enough—

The Grendsluagh jumped back toward its victim from the other side. In one swift, terrible movement, it reached down to claim Emily, its twisted talons closing around her fragile form.

"No!" Walker bellowed, rage and desperation fuelling his every step.

He charged the beast, head down, ready to tackle it.

The Grendsluagh slashed its talons down, carving a deep, painful gash across Walker's body, knocking him to the rocky floor.

But it gave Laurel enough time to reach them.

As the creature lunged once more, she dashed in, thrusting the obsidian talisman at the Grendsluagh.

It reared back, recoiling from the object's power — but as it drew closer to the lava pit, the Grendsluagh seemed to grow in energy once more, drawing strength from the volcano. The surrounding air crackled with its dark force.

It took a step toward Laurel, emboldened by its new potency.

Behind them, Walker reached for Emily and dragged her prone form away, heading for the edge of the chamber, leaving a trail of his own blood in their wake.

With a snarl of rage, the Grendsluagh lunged, its razor-sharp talons slashing through the air.

Laurel cried out as the creature's claws sliced into her flesh.

The blow knocked the talisman from her hand, and the impact sent her crashing against the cavern's rocky wall. She collapsed in a bloody heap, groaning in pain.

Walker stood over Emily as the monster charged with renewed energy, smashing the broken talisman under its feet as it thundered over the cavern floor.

Walker rushed forward with the sword-like femur raised as a weapon. As the monstrous creature swiped at him, Walker deftly darted beneath the sweeping arc of its talons, its claws slicing through the air just above his head.

As he passed beneath its arm, Walker plunged the bone weapon sharply up. He slashed it across the Grendsluagh's torso as he commando-rolled away behind it.

The Grendsluagh spun after him. Thick, black ichor poured from the wound, and it roared with rage and frustration.

With renewed ferocity, it slashed at Walker again and again. It advanced, its talons leaving a trail of destruction across his chest as he desperately tried to back away.

But he had to keep its attention on him.

Behind the Grendsluagh, Laurel crawled slowly toward Emily, every inch hard won. Walker had to give her time to reach his daughter.

As the Grendsluagh swiped again, relentless in its pursuit, Walker darted to one side. He spat out a mouthful of blood as he clutched his wounded side, sensing that something critical was crushed inside. The sand was running out in his hourglass.

The monster was more powerful than he had imagined. Both he and Laurel were too weak to defeat it, even together. Especially now the talisman lay broken in pieces.

It wouldn't be long before it killed him, then devoured Emily and the two women who had followed him to their doom. Its never-ending cycle of violence would continue for another generation.

Walker couldn't let that happen.

The abomination had been born of fire and sacrifice — and it must end that way.

He brandished the sharp femur, keeping the Grendsluagh back as he inched closer to the edge of the lava pit. The heat was unbearable, and the acrid smell of sulphur burned his nostrils. As panic threatened, Walker pushed down the memory of the past, concentrating only on the here and now.

On the far side of the cavern, Laurel reached Emily. With an arm around her torso, the librarian dragged the unconscious young woman toward the tunnel.

Sensing his gaze, Laurel looked up and met Walker's eyes across the cavern.

A look of understanding passed across her features. She shook her head in a desperate no, crying out for him — but Walker couldn't hear her words under the roar of the flames.

As the Grendsluagh advanced once more, he summoned the last of his strength.

Pushing down the pain in his battered, bleeding body,

Walker charged at the Grendsluagh with a primal scream.

He wrapped his arms around the creature's grotesque, pulsating torso and, with every ounce of his remaining power, he drove it backward toward the edge of the lava pit.

The Grendsluagh roared in fury. Its massive limbs flailed wildly, slashing down as it struggled to break free from Walker's grip.

Walker held on and pushed it back, even as the searing heat from the lava pit grew hotter still, as if the air itself was on fire. The surrounding atmosphere shimmered with heat as they wrestled on the very edge of the lava pit, teetering precariously on the brink.

The molten lava below cast eerie, flickering shadows on the cavern walls of man and monster, entwined in a desperate embrace.

With a last surge of strength, Walker hurled himself at his foe — tumbling along with the Grendsluagh into the fiery chasm.

As the scorching lava swallowed him, Walker's final thought was of Emily on stage, performing in *The Tempest*, her eyes bright with hope for the future. A future that would now be free from the shadow of the Grendsluagh.

CHAPTER 26

Laurel watched in horror as Walker and the monster toppled over the edge of the lava pit.

"No!" she screamed, but the roar of flame swallowed her cry.

A plume of fire shot up from the depths. It crackled against the blackened stone above as if the body of the Grendsluagh had imparted all its ferocious energy to the heart of the volcano.

"Laurel?" Max stumbled out of the side tunnel, her injured arm clutched tight against her chest. "What happened? Where's Walker?"

As tears streamed down her face, Laurel could only gesture toward the lava pit.

With realisation dawning, Max knelt down next to her and pulled Laurel into an embrace.

Emily stirred, blinking as her eyes struggled to adjust to the light.

"Dad?" she asked weakly, her voice barely a whisper. She looked from Max to Laurel and then around the cavern. "Where's my dad?"

Laurel shook her head. "He's gone. I'm so sorry. He died to save you, to save us all. He killed the Grendsluagh. It's over."

As the scarlet light from the lava pit danced across their faces, Laurel, Max, and Emily wept together, grieving for the loss of a friend and a father. A hero.

A minute later, the lava in the pit began to boil and spurt violently. It shot flames into the air, as if the death of the Grendsluagh had caused an overload of energy deep in the volcano's heart.

The intense heat ignited the strange lichen and plants that clung to the walls. Fire licked the ceiling of the cave and began to spread.

The air in the cavern grew thick with a suffocating, acrid cloud that filled their lungs and stung their eyes. The temperature skyrocketed, becoming almost unbearable. Sweat poured down their faces, and the heat threatened to overwhelm them.

"We have to get out of here," Max shouted. "The lava pit looks like it might explode, and the cavern is unstable."

She pointed at a tunnel around to their left. "That must be the route the Grendsluagh took from the Cavern of Offering. It should give us a faster way back to the surface."

Laurel and Max helped Emily up, the three of them battered and bruised but determined to honour Walker's sacrifice by making it out of the depths alive.

They staggered up and out as the walls of the cavern were consumed by the ravenous flames. The heat was so intense that the air seemed to shimmer and warp as the hellish inferno chased them up through the tunnel.

The ground trembled beneath their feet, and the walls of the cavern shook, threatening to collapse at any moment. Exhausted and racked with grief, they stumbled on, up and away from the catacomb.

As their desperate footsteps echoed through the ancient passageway, Laurel was grateful for Max's knowledge of the caves. The urbexer skilfully guided them through the twists and turns of the labyrinthine tunnels, even as their vision was blurred by the smoke and tears that filled their eyes.

At last, the three crawled out of a covered entrance of a side tunnel in Holyrood Park. They were covered in soot and blood and bone dust. They were broken, injured, and grieving — but they were alive.

As the coral streaks of dawn lit the sky, they sat gasping on the side of Arthur's Seat, staring from the hill down at the city below.

With a sudden blast of heat and a boom of exploding energy, a pillar of flame shot up from the depths, engulfing the university library at the heart of the Cabal's empire.

The wail of sirens echoed from the streets as fire services converged on the scene. Soon, a press helicopter hovered overhead.

But the firefighters couldn't stop the blaze.

As Laurel, Max, and Emily watched from on high, the ancient structure crumbled and collapsed under the intense heat, sending plumes of smoke and ash into the sky.

The once-majestic building was reduced to a smouldering ruin, signalling the end of the Cabal's reign over Edinburgh. There would be no further sacrifices to the monster of the depths.

Laurel didn't know what that meant for the prosperity of the city, but now it was no longer plagued by the shadow of the Grendsluagh. It was free to heal and rebuild. Just as the three of them would do, in memory of Walker Kane.

ENJOYED CATACOMB?

If you loved the story, I would really appreciate a short review on your preferred site.

Your help in spreading the word is gratefully appreciated and reviews make a huge difference to help new readers find my books. Thank you!

Join my fiction Reader's Group and get a free thriller ebook

You'll also be notified of new releases, giveaways and receive personal updates from behind the scenes of my books and photos from my research trips. Sign up at:

www.JFPenn.com/free

Books and Travel Podcast

Interviews and solo episodes about the deeper side of books and travel. Available on your favourite podcast app. Find the backlist episodes at:

www.BooksAndTravel.page/listen

ABOUT J.F. PENN

J.F. Penn is the Award-nominated, New York Times and USA Today bestselling author of the ARKANE action adventure thrillers, Brooke & Daniel psychological/crime thrillers, and the Mapwalker fantasy adventure series, as well as other standalone stories.

Her books weave together ancient artifacts, relics of power, international locations, and adventure with an edge of the supernatural.

Jo lives in Bath, England with her husband and two British shorthair cats, Cashew and Noisette. She enjoys a nice G&T.

* * *

Sign up for your free thriller, *Day of the Vikings*, and receive updates from behind the scenes, research, and giveaways at:

www.jfpenn.com/free

Buy books direct:
www.JFPennBooks.com

* * *

Connect with Joanna:
www.JFPenn.com
joanna@JFPenn.com
www.Facebook.com/JFPennAuthor
www.Instagram.com/JFPennAuthor
www.BooksAndTravel.page

* * *

For writers:

Jo's site, www.TheCreativePenn.com empowers authors with the knowledge they need to choose their creative future. Books and courses, as well as her award-winning show, *The Creative Penn Podcast*, provide information and inspiration on writing craft and business.

MORE BOOKS BY J.F. PENN

You can find all my books as well as special editions, bundles and book stacks at www.JFPennBooks.com and also on your favourite online bookstore in all the usual formats.

ARKANE Action-Adventure Thrillers

Stone of Fire #1
Crypt of Bone #2
Ark of Blood #3
One Day in Budapest #4
Day of the Vikings #5
Gates of Hell #6
One Day in New York #7
Destroyer of Worlds #8
End of Days #9
Valley of Dry Bones #10
Tree of Life #11
Tomb of Relics #12
Short story: Soldiers of God

Brooke and Daniel Psychological/Crime Thrillers

Desecration #1
Delirium #2
Deviance #3

Mapwalker Dark Fantasy Adventures

Map of Shadows #1
Map of Plagues #2
Map of the Impossible #3

Short Stories

A Thousand Fiendish Angels
The Dark Queen
Blood, Sweat, and Flame
A Midwinter Sacrifice

Other Books

Risen Gods — co-written with J. Thorn

American Demon Hunters: Sacrifice — co-written with J. Thorn, Lindsay Buroker, and Zach Bohannon

AUTHOR'S NOTE

I visited the vaults under Edinburgh over a decade ago and I knew one day I would set a story there. I hope you enjoyed *Catacomb*!

How far will a father go to save his daughter?

I wanted to write something like the movie *Taken* (2008) with Liam Neeson as a monster book with an almost mythical hero in the vein of Beowulf. I also wanted an emotional ending like the movie *Armageddon* (1998) with Bruce Willis, where he sacrifices himself for his daughter's happiness.

The Grendsluagh is an amalgamation of Grendel, the monster that Beowulf fought and the Sluagh, restless spirits of the dead from Celtic myth.

Research and Bibliography

If you visit Edinburgh, go on an Underground Vaults and Graveyard Tour. There are lots of them, some at night and some with an emphasis on the supernatural …

I read a lot of books for research. Inspiration for this story included:

> *Writing Monsters: How to Craft Believably Terrifying Creatures to Enhance Your Horror, Fantasy, and Science Fiction* — Philip Athans

Explore Everything: Place-Hacking the City — Bradley L. Garrett

Access All Areas: A User's Guide to the Art of Urban Exploration — Ninjalicious

Edinburgh After Dark: Vampires, Ghosts, and Witches of the Old Town — Ron Halliday

USE OF AI AND OTHER TOOLS

In an age where more content is generated with AI tools and many jobs are increasingly AI-assisted, I think it's important to state usage in my books.

I'm a techno-optimist and believe that AI tools driven by human decisions and guided by human hands can augment creativity. I've used technology as part of my creative and business processes for the last 15 years and consider AI tools as the latest wave.

For *Catacomb*, I used Google for research, ChatGPT as part of the creative process, and ProWritingAid as part of my editing process before sending to my (human) editor, Kristen. I use Amazon for publishing, and Amazon auto-ads, as well as Facebook/Meta for marketing, and social media sites, which are all powered by AI.

I used Midjourney to create images to inspire scenes in the book, which I use in social media and marketing. My (human) designer, Jane, used some images as part of the composite book cover.

ACKNOWLEDGMENTS

Thanks as ever to my readers and Pennfriends.

Thanks to my editor, Kristen Tate at The Blue Garret, and my book designer, Jane Dixon Smith for cover and interior design.

Printed in Great Britain
by Amazon